CLAUDIA AND THE BAD JOKE

**Other books by
Ann M. Martin**

8.A

Rachel Parker, Kindergarten Show-off
Eleven Kids, One Summer
Ma and Pa Dracula
Yours Turly, Shirley
Ten Kids, No Pets
Slam Book
Just a Summer Romance
Missing Since Monday
With You and Without You
Me and Katie (the Pest)
Stage Fright
Inside Out
Bummer Summer

BABY-SITTERS LITTLE SISTER series
THE BABY-SITTERS CLUB mysteries
THE BABY-SITTERS CLUB series

CLAUDIA AND THE BAD JOKE

Ann M. Martin

AN
APPLE
PAPERBACK

SCHOLASTIC INC.
New York Toronto London Auckland Sydney

This book is in memory of
Lyman Chamberlain Martin
— Grandpoppy —
who always liked a good joke.

Cover art by Hodges Soileau

ISBN 0-590-60671-9

12 11 10 9 8 7 6 5 4 3 2 1   1   6 7 8 9/9 0 1/0

Printed in the U.S.A.   40

CHAPTER 1

"You know," said Kristy Thomas, "I have never been hit in the face with a pie."

"Imagine that," I teased her. "Sweet thirteen and never been hit. What a tragedy."

My friends and I laughed.

"Well, personally," said Jessi Ramsey, "I would not want to be hit in the face with a pie, thank you very much."

"I don't know," said Jessi's best friend, Mallory Pike. "It would depend on the kind of pie."

"Yeah," agreed Kristy. "A double chocolate pie wouldn't be bad at all. Besides, there's always the attraction of *wearing* food."

Logan Bruno looked at Kristy as if she were crazy. He was the only boy among us. Therefore, he had never been at one of our Baby-sitters Club slumber parties, which explains why he didn't know about Kristy's food theory. The thing is, Kristy has always thought it would

1

be kind of cool to wear food. Like, to hang grapes from your earlobes, or make a vest out of teabags.

Mary Anne Spier began to turn green, which often happens when Kristy starts in on food. Mary Anne has a weak stomach and Kristy has a big mouth.

"I," said Dawn Schafer, "would only want to get hit with — "

"We know, we know," I jumped in. "An all-natural, sugar-free pie. Well, *I* wouldn't mind getting hit with any kind of pie."

"I'll keep that in mind," Logan told me.

"SHH! *SHH!* Quiet down, everybody. Find your seats."

It was a rainy Saturday afternoon. My friends and I had been bored out of our minds — until Logan (who happens to be Mary Anne's boyfriend) called her to say that there was going to be a slapstick film festival at the public library. That in itself was pretty good. Better yet, it was free.

Mary Anne agreed to go. She didn't have to think twice (although she did have to check with her father, who's on the strict side). Then she called Kristy and Dawn, her best friends, to tell them about the film festival; Kristy called me; Dawn called Mallory; Mallory called Jessi; and a few hours later we were sitting in the

2

meeting room at the Stoneybrook Public Library having a conversation about wearing food and throwing pies. It was intermission. We had seen three short, very silly films. Now intermission was over and it was time for two more.

I looked around the room as the lights dimmed. It seemed that all of Stoneybrook was there. (Well, all of Stoneybrook under sixteen.) I saw a bunch of Mallory's brothers and sisters, Jessi's younger sister, Kristy's little brother, and a lot of the kids my friends and I baby-sit for.

My friends and I, by the way, are more than just friends. We're the members of a club that Kristy started — the Baby-sitters Club. There's Kristy Thomas, Mary Anne Spier, Dawn Schafer, Jessi Ramsey, Mallory Pike, and me, Claudia Kishi. (Logan Bruno is not a true member of the club. He and a friend of Kristy's, Shannon Kilbourne, are associate members. More about that later.)

Ka-BOOM!

Ha, ha, ha. Hee, hee, hee. A new movie was on, and a guy on the screen was having a birthday. Someone had just set a beautiful cake in front of him. Really, it was a work of art. Bunches of candy roses and garlands of frosting flowers decorated it. The guy leaned over to blow out the candles and — *POW!* The cake exploded! Everyone in the room was laughing hysterically. The poor guy was now wearing the cake.

I turned to look at Kristy. She was enthralled. I'm sure she was imagining herself with buttercream eyelashes and hair.

Kristy and her ideas. Kristy amazes me. Her mind is always working, working. She thinks up lots of great ideas. That's why she's the president of the Baby-sitters Club. Kristy used to live across the street from me here in Stoneybrook, Connecticut. And Mary Anne lived in the house next door to her. (Well, she still lives there.) So the three of us pretty much grew up together. Despite that, it's hard to imagine three more different people. Let me tell you about us.

I'll start with Kristy, since you already know about her big ideas. Kristy is thirteen, just like Mary Anne, Dawn, Logan, and me. (Mal and Jessi are eleven.) But sometimes she seems younger than the rest of us eighth-graders. A little less mature, I guess. She's the shortest kid in our grade (which is not her fault), she's a tomboy, and she doesn't care much about clothes. Or boys. She always wears the same kind of outfit — blue jeans, running shoes, a turtleneck, and a sweater. There's nothing wrong with that, but there *are* other things to wear. I mean, she could try a floppy bow in her hair or some interesting ponytail holders, or some big earrings. That's what I would do. But then, I'm not Kristy.

Kristy has an interesting family. And the last year in her life, in terms of family, hasn't been easy. When Kristy lived across the street from me, she lived with her mom, her older brothers Charlie (he's seventeen) and Sam (fifteen), and her little brother, David Michael, who's seven. Kristy's dad left the Thomases a long time ago and they pretty much never hear from him. Sometimes Kristy gets mad about that. I mean, would it kill her father to remember her birthday by sending a card? Anyway, Kristy's mother met this millionaire, Watson Brewer, and fell in love with him. They got married last summer, and Watson moved Kristy and her family across town to his mansion. So Kristy moved, got a stepfather, and also got a stepbrother and stepsister all in a short period of time. Andrew and Karen are her steps. They're four and six, and Kristy loves them to bits, even though she only sees them every other weekend. (Mostly, they live with their mother, Watson's first wife.) Also, somewhere in all of this, the Thomases' wonderful old collie, Louie, had to be put to sleep. Kristy seems to have survived everything, though.

I'm not sure Mary Anne could have. As I mentioned before, Kristy and Mary Anne are best friends. They have been practically since they were born. And they're a pretty good example of the saying that opposites attract. Kristy is tough and has a big mouth. Mary Anne is sensitive, shy, and quiet (although I think she's coming out of her shell). Mary Anne is also a good listener, a fair person, and a romantic who will cry at anything. She used to be like Kristy in that she was very short and didn't care about clothes, but lately she's grown a few inches and has taken *much* more interest in her wardrobe. She's definitely getting trendier.

Mary Anne lives with her dad and her kitten, Tigger. Her mom died when Mary Anne was just a little kid. Since Mr. Spier had to raise her by himself, he was much too strict with her for the longest time. Now he's getting better. (Luckily, he likes Logan.)

Then there's me. I am soooo different from Mary Anne and Kristy. For starters, I'm Japanese-American. Also, I love to mess around with clothes and jewelry. I might as well just come out and say it — I'm one of the coolest-looking kids in Stoneybrook Middle School. I know that sounds conceited, but everyone agrees it's true. I wear wild clothes, such as baggy pants and sweaters, high-top sneakers, and jewelry I make myself. For instance, at the film festival, I was wearing earrings made of wooden beads that I'd painted. My hair is long and jet-black, and I'm always experimenting with different ways to fix it or decorate it.

Kristy's hobby is sports, Mary Anne's is needlework, mine is art. I just love art — painting, drawing, sketching, collage-making — and crafts, too. I'm addicted to junk food, and I love to read Nancy Drew mysteries, but I'm a terrible student. This is too bad, since my older sister, Janine, is a genius. She's a high-school student who takes college courses. Janine and I live with our parents and Mimi, the most wonderful grandmother in the world.

What about Dawn, Jessi, and Mal? Well, I won't forget to tell you what they're like. I'll start with Dawn. She's Mary Anne's other best friend. Dawn moved here less than a year ago and she and Mary Anne became friends right away, which was a little hard on Kristy. Dawn moved all the way across the United States from California with her mother and her younger brother, Jeff. They moved because her parents had just gotten divorced, and Mrs. Schafer

7

wanted to come back to Stoneybrook, which was where she'd grown up. The divorce and the move were quite a change for all the Schafers, especially Jeff, who finally decided he couldn't take the East Coast. So not long ago, he moved back to his dad. Dawn won't do that, though. She's a California girl, all right (she hates junk food, red meat, and cold weather), but she's extremely close to her mother. So she's staying.

Talk about survivors, Dawn is a champion one. She's an individual, too. She stands up for what she believes in, even when no one else believes in it, and she dresses the way she pleases, and does things her own way. She's not stuck-up, though, and she doesn't step all over people, trying to get her own way. In fact, she's one of the nicest people I know. Dawn is a good student, she's addicted to ghost stories the way I'm addicted to junk food and Nancy Drew books — and she lives in a house with a *real* secret passage in it.

Now on to our younger club members, Mal and Jessi. Mal used to be someone our club sat *for*. She's the oldest of the eight Pike kids. But as last year went on, we noticed that whenever we sat for the Pikes, Mal was much more of a sit*ter* than a sit*tee*. So when one of our members had to drop out of the club (more about that later), we asked Mal, and later Jessi, too, to fill her spot. I think the thing I like most about Mallory is that she's so practical and levelheaded. You could say to her, "Mal, there's a lion loose in the basement," and she'd say, perfectly calmly, "Okay, close the basement door, call nine-one-one, and evacuate the children. And don't anybody take any meat out of the refrigerator."

Mallory wants desperately to grow up and to look older. I think it's her mission in life. She wants her parents to say she can get pierced ears instead of braces. She wants her freckles to go away and her curly hair to straighten out. And she wants contact lenses instead of glasses. Mallory loves reading and writing and might become an author one day. She's not sure yet. Right now, she'd settle for getting a miniskirt and a glittery sweat shirt (just two of the things her parents say she's not old enough for).

Jessi (short for Jessica) Ramsey is Mallory's best friend, even though the Ramseys have lived in Stoneybrook for a very short time. She and Mal found each other when they needed best friends. Also, they have lots in common, so they just hit it off. Like Mal, Jessi loves to read, and they both especially love horse stories. Plus, Jessi is a terrific dancer — a ballerina.

Although she doesn't plan to become a dancer professionally, she goes to the best ballet school in the area (in Stamford, the nearest city). Also like Mal, Jessi thinks her parents treat her like a little kid, and *she's* getting braces, not pierced ears, and has to wear glasses (just for reading, though). Jessi told me that if once, just once, she could wear clothes like mine to school, she could die happy.

Jessi lives with her mom, her dad, her eight-year-old sister, Becca (short for Rebecca), and her baby brother, Squirt. Squirt's real name is John Philip Ramsey, Jr., and he's adorable.

Oh, one other thing about the Ramseys which I guess I should mention. They're black, one of the few black families in town. And the people of Stoneybrook (well, *some* of the people of Stoneybrook) sure didn't make them feel welcome at first. But Jessi says things are getting better now. Thank goodness. As my dad would say, though, we all have our crosses to bear. That means, we all have problems.

And as I looked around at the members of the club, I thought how true that was. Each of us did have our own problems. But at that moment, no one was thinking about them. We were giggling and laughing instead.

On the movie screen, a man dressed in a tux was holding out a corsage to a woman in an evening gown. The woman leaned over to smell the flowers and *SPLAT!* A stream of water got her right in the eye.

But just then, the man got hit in the face with a coconut cream pie.

"Awesome!" whispered Kristy. "That's my dream!"

The movie ended, the lights were turned on, and we stood up. The film fest was over. What none of us knew then was that a practical joke fest was about to begin.

CHAPTER 2

I was under my bed. My head was, anyway. I was looking for a bag of Doritos that I *knew* I had hidden there. Remember when I said I love junk food? What I didn't mention was that my parents don't approve of eating a lot of the stuff, so I have to hide it in my room. It's everywhere — but you'd never know it. The naked eye cannot see it. Well, the naked eye cannot see it unless it knows where to look. There was a Butterfinger bar in the drawer of my jewelry box, a package of Double-Stuff Oreos in a shoebox labeled PANT BRUSHES (so I'm not a great speller, okay?), and I knew — I just *knew* — there was a bag of Doritos somewhere under the bed. Only I couldn't find it.

I wanted to find it in the next ten minutes. It was 5:20. At five-thirty a meeting of the Baby-sitters Club was going to start, and I like to be prepared with a little food, because we're all usually starving by this time of day.

It was a shame my room was such a mess. I mean, I'd like it to be a little neater since my friends spend so much time in it. But I can't help being messy. I need to save things that I can use in my art projects, plus I store canvasses and brushes and charcoals and pastels all over the place. The good thing about a mess, though, is that it helps you hide stuff, like junk food. Also, like Nancy Drew mysteries. I have to hide *those* because my parents think I should be reading more worthwhile books. I can't think what they would be.

"Ah-*ha!* There you are!" I exclaimed. I saw my Doritos behind a pillow and some other things that had somehow wound up under the bed.

"Hi, Claud!"

"Ow!" I replied, as I banged my head on the bed, trying to scramble out.

Dawn had arrived. Mimi must have let her in. Mimi knows my friends, and they love her as much as I do. She loves them right back. That's just the kind of person Mimi is.

"Sorry," said Dawn. "I didn't mean to scare you. I'm a little early."

"That's okay," I answered. I sat up and rubbed my head. Then I held out the Doritos. "I knew these were under there somewhere."

Dawn wrinkled her nose, plainly meaning, "Junk food. Ew."

Kristy showed up then. Since her move across town, she depends on her brother Charlie to drive her to and from meetings. (The club pays him for this, in order to be sure that he'll do it regularly.) Kristy headed straight for my director's chair — she conducts our meetings from it — put her visor on, stuck a pencil over one ear, and reached for the club notebook.

She was ready.

The time was 5:25. Within the next five minutes, Mary Anne, Jessi, and Mal showed up. The club members are prompt. Kristy wouldn't have it any other way.

Maybe I should explain to you how our club works. I better start by telling you how Kristy got the idea for it. One evening her mother said that she was going to need a sitter for David Michael. It turned out that she needed one at a time when none of the older Thomas kids — not Charlie, not Sam, not Kristy — was available. So Mrs. Thomas got on the phone and started making calls. It took forever to find a sitter.

While that was going on, Kristy was thinking how terrific it would be if her mother could make just one call and get in touch with a whole lot of sitters at once. And that was the beginning of the Baby-sitters Club. Kristy got together with Mary Anne, me, and another girl, Stacey McGill. (Stacey's the one who had to move away, the one Jessi and Mallory replaced.) The four of us decided to meet on Monday, Wednesday, and Friday afternoons from five-thirty until six. We did plenty of advertising so people would know when we were meeting and could call us at those times.

Kristy's idea was terrific. People did call us. They always reached four sitters, and at least one of us was usually available to take their jobs. Our clients loved finding sitters so fast, and we loved our baby-sitting jobs and earning money.

Since then, the club and the way it's run haven't changed much, but the members have. First, Dawn moved here and joined us, becoming the fifth member. Then Stacey had to move away. That was *really* sad (for me) since Stacey and I had gotten to be friends. In fact, she was my first and only best friend. She's been gone for awhile now, and I miss her a lot. But she's not *too* far away — just in New York City — so we talk on the phone a lot, and recently Mary Anne, Dawn, Kristy, and I visited her there and stayed for the weekend!

Anyway, by the time Stacey left, our club

was doing so much business that we knew we'd have to replace her. First we found Mal, which was good but not good enough, because Mal is too young to sit in the evening, unless she's helping take care of her own brothers and sisters. So we asked Jessi to join, too. She's not allowed to sit in the evening, either, but we figured two afternoon-only sitters would free up the rest of us enough to handle the evening jobs. So far, we seem to be right. Plus, we have Logan and Shannon as backups. We call one of them when the club is offered a job that none of us can take.

Logan and Shannon, as I said earlier, are associate members of the club, meaning that they don't attend meetings. Mal and Jessi are junior members. The rest of us hold offices. You know about Kristy's. Her office is president. As president, she gets great ideas, conducts the meetings, and generally keeps things running.

I'm the vice-president. That's because we hold the club meetings in my room, and *that's* because I'm lucky enough to have my own phone and personal, private phone number. When job calls come in, which is often, we don't tie up anyone else's line.

Mary Anne is the club secretary. She probably does more actual work for the club than the rest of us put together. You see, it's the job of the secretary to keep the club record book in order and up-to-date. The record book is one of the two most important features of the club. (I'll tell you about the other one in a minute.) It's where Mary Anne writes down the names and addresses of our clients, it's where Dawn (our treasurer) keeps track of the money we earn, *and* it's where Mary Anne schedules our baby-sitting jobs. That is not easy to do. Mary Anne has to remember all sorts of things, like when Jessi goes to her ballet lessons or when I go to my art classes, in order to know when we're free to sit. Somehow, she keeps everything straight, though. The appointment calendar in the book is always accurate and contains the latest information. Thank goodness for Mary Anne.

I might as well tell you about the other important feature of the club now, while I'm on the subject. It's the notebook we keep. This, of course, was Kristy's idea. None of the rest of us would have thought of it, and none of the rest of us like writing in it very much — but we all admit that it's helpful. In the notebook, each of us is supposed to describe *every* job we go on, even if the job is, say, Mallory taking care of some of her own brothers and sisters. It's surprising what we can learn by reading about our friends' sitting experiences. Plus, it's just good to know what's going on with the kids we sit for. Anyway, we write up our jobs, and then we're responsible for reading the notebook once a week. We keep the record book and notebook in my room, the club headquarters.

The fourth office in our club is treasurer, and that belongs to Dawn. Dawn took over the job from Stacey when Stacey moved. Stacey had been a great treasurer. She loves numbers and is a real math brain. Dawn is just average at math, but she's doing a fine job. She keeps careful records of who earns how much money, and she watches over the treasury, always remembering to collect dues, to give Kristy money to pay Charlie, and to let us know when club funds are getting low. And that's about it. I can't think of much else to tell you, so I'll just let you see how a typical meeting is run.

Kristy began it at five-thirty on the nose.

"Any urgent club business?" she asked.

We shook our heads. We'd been busy, but things had been running smoothly.

"The treasury is fine," Dawn spoke up. "We've got plenty of money to pay Charlie, and more left over in case anyone needs anything for her Kid-Kit."

Oops. I forgot to tell you about Kid-Kits. Kristy thought those up too. Naturally. They're boxes that we decorated and keep filled with our old toys, books, and games, plus a few new items such as coloring books or activity books. We each have one, and sometimes we bring them with us when we baby-sit. The Kid-Kits are always a surprise and always a treat. Children love them!

We were discussing what we needed for our Kid-Kits when the phone rang. Jessi answered it, and Mary Anne, record book open, set up a job for Dawn. As soon as she hung up, it rang again. Mrs. Perkins, whose family moved into Kristy's old house, was calling to say she needed a sitter for Myriah and Gabbie. Then two more of our regular customers called.

We had just arranged sitters for *those* jobs, when the phone rang a fifth time. Kristy answered it. After saying yes a lot, asking a bunch of questions, and nodding her head, she told the caller, "I'll get right back to you." Kristy hung up. "Okay," she said to us club members, "a new client. Mrs. Sobak. She lives on Cherry Valley Road. She needs a sitter for her eight-year-old daughter, Betsy, this Thursday afternoon."

Mary Anne was looking at our calendar. "Claudia, you're free," she said.

"Great," I replied. "But I'm confused. I know other kids in that neighborhood who sit for Betsy Sobak. How come her mother is calling *us?*"

Kristy shrugged. "Don't knock it," she said. "A job is a job. Mrs. Sobak's regular sitters are probably all busy. Maybe the Sobaks will become regular clients."

"Right," I agreed.

Kristy called Mrs. Sobak and told her that I would be Betsy's sitter. When she hung up, she looked at her watch. "Almost six," she announced. "Oh, hey, Mary Anne, can I have the record book for a sec?"

"Sure," replied Mary Anne. She leaned over, holding the book out.

Kristy reached for it, pen in hand, and *SPLOOTCH.* She squirted blue ink all over Mary Anne's white sweat shirt. Mary Anne gasped, but Kristy dissolved in laughter. "It's disappearing ink!" she cried. "Sam lent it to me!"

We all watched the ink disappear, but Kristy was the only one laughing. Somehow, a practical joke seemed funnier in the movies than in real life.

CHAPTER 3

The meeting ended at six o'clock, but it was six-fifteen before all of my friends had drifted away. Dawn was the last to leave. With her brother Jeff back in California, Dawn's never in a rush to get home. She might be if she thought her mother would be there, but Mrs. Schafer works very hard at her job and recently hasn't been getting home until seven on weeknights. And sometimes she goes out with this guy, Trip, whom Dawn calls the Trip-Man and can't stand. Dawn has stayed over at our house for supper a few times, but that night, she headed home to start fixing dinner.

I went downstairs to give Mimi a hand with our own dinner. I found her in the kitchen making a salad. I could smell chicken cooking.

"Hello, my Claudia," she greeted me. "How was meeting?"

Mimi is native Japanese (English is her second language), but the reason she talks funny doesn't have anything to do with that. It's because she had a stroke last summer. The stroke left her with a limp, and she can't use her right hand. Also, she has trouble with her speech. Even so, my family is amazed at how much she's relearned in the past few months.

I kissed Mimi on the cheek. "The meeting was fine," I told her. "Oh, I think we have a new client. Mrs. Sobak. She needed a sitter for her daughter, and I got the job. I go on Thursday."

"Wonderful!" said Mimi.

"What can I do to help?" I asked.

Words must have escaped Mimi just then, because all she did was point into the dining room. I knew she wanted me to set the table.

I had just finished, when the genius came home.

"Hello," she said somberly.

I guess life is a trial when you're as smart as my sister Janine. All I worry about is baby-sitting and art projects. And maybe school. Janine has to worry about molecular theories and foreign politics and things like, Will the earth ever revolve so near the sun that it burns up?

My parents came home not long after Janine, and since Mimi's dinner was ready, we sat down to eat.

"How was school?" Dad asked when we'd all been served.

I was hoping he was asking Janine, but no, he was looking at me.

Darn. That simple question can be very touchy.

"Fine," I replied.

"Did you get your math quiz back?" Janine wanted to know.

I shot her a killer look, but everyone was waiting for my answer. They had all helped me study for that quiz.

"Yes," I answered.

Silence.

"And how did you do?" Mom finally asked.

"I got, um, an eighty-one." I put a huge bite of chicken in my mouth, hoping no one would ask me questions when they could see that I was trying to chew.

No one did. More silence.

I swallowed my chicken. I sighed. "An eighty-one," I told them, "is good. It's a B-minus."

Mimi smiled at me from across the table. She didn't say anything, though, and this time it wasn't because of her stroke. It was because she and my parents don't agree on my school-work. My parents think I could try harder and do better; Mimi thinks they should leave me alone. But Mimi isn't my mother, so she doesn't say anything.

I changed the subject in what I thought was a very kind and thoughtful way. "Tell us about your research project," I said to Janine.

Janine's projects are all boring, so I hardly ever ask about them. However, Janine loves to talk about them. She was flattered that I'd asked. I was relieved that she had something long-winded to say.

The attention was off of me and my B-minus (which, frankly, I'd been sort of proud of).

When dinner was over, Mom and Dad and Janine cleared the table and began cleaning the kitchen. Mimi and I went into the living room to do my homework. It's sort of a family rule that somebody has to give me a hand with my homework each night. This is because my grades used to be so bad. My homework was always a mess, and I didn't know how to study for tests or quizzes. The best homework nights are the ones on which Mimi helps me. The worst are the ones on which Janine helps me. I wish I didn't have to have any help at all, but my parents told me I couldn't stay in the Baby-sitters Club unless I kept my grades up.

"All right," Mimi began, "what are your assign — assign — what is homework?"

"One page of math problems, read this chapter in my science book, and answer these questions for English," I told her.

Mimi nodded. "Where to start?"

"English," I said promptly. I don't love English, but I *hate* math and science.

"Why not get bad work done first, then do English?" suggested Mimi.

I screwed up my face. "Okay," I agreed.

We began with the math. I don't know what it is about numbers. They just don't make sense to me. Stacey once said that she can "read" numbers the way she can read words. She understands them. She can look at a problem for a few moments, and suddenly she has the answer, without doing any figuring or writing. She calculates things in her head as if her brain were a computer.

Not me. Oh, no. I sit and figure, and half the time I'm figuring wrong. Adding when I should be multiplying, subtracting four from ten and getting seven. What a mess!

Mimi and I plodded through my work. Mimi is *so* patient. She never raises her voice or gets aggravated.

"Now," she said, when I had finished my math and science, "where are English plobrems, my Claudia?"

I knew she had meant to say "problems." "They're just some questions," I told her, "and they're right here."

In English class this year we're reading the Newbery Award-winning books. We've already read several. Now we're reading *Roll of Thunder, Hear My Cry*. I didn't think I would like it, but really, it isn't bad.

Mimi looked at the list of questions and read the first one. "In what — in what ways is main — is *the* main character in *Roll of*, um, *Thunder, Hear My Cry* simi — similar to main — to *the* main character in *A Wrinkle in Time*?"

"Oh, lord," I replied, "They couldn't be more different! I hate questions like that."

"Think, my Claudia. Is *any*thing the same about them?"

"They're both girls," I said.

If Janine had been helping me, she probably would have thrown down her pencil in disgust at that answer, but Mimi just said, "That a good start. What else?"

We worked and worked. The more we talked, the more answers I found. When we were finally done, I kissed Mimi, thanked her, and escaped to my room.

Ah, art. I looked at the half-finished pastel drawing on my easel. I just stood in front of it for several minutes, thinking. After awhile,

I opened my box of pastels and slowly set to work. When I'm in the middle of a good project, especially a painting or a drawing, I can forget about everything else. Which is what I did. And which may explain why I jumped a mile when the phone rang.

"Hello?" I said.

"Hi, Claudia. It's Ashley."

Ashley Wyeth is a new friend of mine. We have a funny relationship. It seems like we're always mad at each other. We're forever fighting, then making up. But Ashley is the only person who truly understands my love of art. She's an artist herself — the most talented person our age I know. Before she moved to Stoneybrook, she lived in Chicago and went to this really great art school there. And *she* thinks *I'm* talented! Ashley can be a pain in the neck, though, because she's always bugging me to quit baby-sitting and spend more time on my art.

So when Ashley called, I braced myself for a lecture, but all she wanted was our English assignment. I read her the questions and then hung up. As soon as I did, the phone rang again.

"Hello?"

At first there was just silence at the other end of the phone. Then an odd-sounding voice said, "Do you have Prince Albert in a can?"

"Huh?" I replied. "Prince Albert?"

"Oh, never mind." The voice suddenly sounded disgusted and the caller hung up.

I looked at the receiver as if it could explain to me what had just happened. A goof call gone wrong, I decided as I hung up. The caller was probably someone who'd been at the film festival. Practical-joke season had begun — and I, for one, did not like it.

CHAPTER 4

It was Thursday morning and I was nervous. A couple of kids who used to baby-sit for Betsy Sobak had told me why they wouldn't do it anymore.

"She's an incurable practical joker," Diana Roberts said.

"Well, she *used* to be," Gordon Brown corrected her. "Supposedly she outgrew it, but I don't sit for her anymore."

"Me neither," agreed Diana. "I don't think it's safe yet."

"I'll let you know," I told them. "Her parents must have gotten desperate without you guys, because her mom called the Baby-sitters Club. I'm going to sit for Betsy this afternoon."

I was smiling, trying to pretend I wasn't nervous. This wasn't easy with Diana and Gordon looking at me sympathetically, but I put up a good front.

"Be careful," Diana called as she headed for the girls' room.

"Yeah, we'll be thinking of you," Gordon added.

Oh, lord. What had I gotten myself into?

I found out at three-thirty that afternoon. That was when I rang the Sobaks' doorbell. I stood nervously on their front stoop. In a moment, the door was opened by a friendly looking girl with brown hair, which had been pulled into two ponytails and tied with big blue ribbons. She was wearing a very snazzy pair of red pants that were held up by red suspenders. Under the suspenders was a blue-and-white-striped T-shirt. The legs of her pants ended in cuffs, and on her feet were running shoes tied with purple laces.

"Hi!" she said cheerfully. "I'm Betsy. Are you Claudia?"

This was the kid I'd been afraid of?

"That's right," I told her. "Claudia Kishi."

"Come on in."

Betsy held the door open for me and I entered the Sobaks' front hallway. A woman bustled forward to meet me, trying to put on her coat and shake my hand at the same time.

"Cookie Sobak," she said. (*Cookie?*) "On my way to a meeting at the Woman's Club. About to be late. Emergency numbers by the phone in the kitchen. Mr. Sobak works at Tile Corp., if you need to reach him. Better fly. Betsy — *behave.* Back at six. Ta-ta.''

''Ta-ta,'' replied Betsy. Then she stuck her tongue out at her mother's back.

''Betsy,'' I admonished her, but I couldn't help smiling. Mrs. Sobak was so, I don't know, *fake,* that I kind of wanted to stick my own tongue out at her.

''Listen,'' I said to Betsy as her mother's car backed down the driveway, ''have you had a snack yet?''

''Um, no. No, I haven't.'' A smile crept over Betsy's face. (I was glad she was so easy to please.) ''Want some cookies?'' she asked. ''My mom makes great oatmeal raisin cookies.''

''Sure,'' I replied. (Oh, goody. Cookies.) ''Here, let me help you.''

''No, no,'' said Betsy hurriedly as she led me into the kitchen. ''You're kind of like my guest. I'll serve us. Do you want some apple juice?''

I didn't, really, but I said yes anyway. Betsy seemed so pleased to be in charge of fixing our snack.

''You sit right there,'' she told me, pointing to a chair at the kitchen table.

I sat. Betsy got busy filling glasses, opening the cookie jar, finding napkins.

"So," I said, "you're an only child, huh, Betsy?"

"Almost," she replied, her back turned. "My sister Pat is twenty-three. She even has a baby. I'm an aunt now."

"Wow," I replied, impressed. I didn't know any other eight-year-old aunts. "Aunt Betsy."

"Yup. Here you go." Betsy set a plate of cookies and two napkins on the table. Then she carefully handed me a tall glass of juice. At last she sat down, a much smaller glass in her hands.

I reached for a cookie. "Mmm," I said, after I'd taken a bite. "These are great. Your mother must be a good cook."

"The best," agreed Betsy.

I took a swallow of apple juice, wishing Betsy hadn't poured me quite so much. There was an awful lot of juice in the glass, and —

"Oh, ew! *Ew!*" I shrieked. Something else was in the glass. A fly! It was stuck in an ice cube!

I'd barely gotten the first "Ew!" out when I realized the glass was dripping. Apple juice was running down my shirt.

"What — ?" I cried. I set the glass on the

table. "Betsy, there's a fly in my glass, and I think . . ."

I stopped talking because Betsy didn't seem the least bit horrified. In fact, she was laughing. Hysterically.

When she got control of herself, she managed to gasp out, "Gotcha! The fly is fake. It's in a fake ice cube! And I gave you a dribble glass!"

"Well, that's just great, Betsy," I said. I knew that, as a baby-sitter, I wasn't supposed to get sarcastic, but *sheesh.* "Now, I've got apple juice all over my white shirt," I told her.

Betsy couldn't have known it, but the shirt was one I'd made myself. I'd taken a shirt of my dad's, painted it, and sewn sequins all over it. It had taken ages to do, and the shirt was very special to me. Also, it had to be dry cleaned.

"Dry cleaning," I informed Betsy, "is expensive. Plus, I'm going to smell like sour apples all afternoon." Practical jokes were seeming less and less funny.

"Sorry," said Betsy, not sounding sorry at all.

"I talked to a couple of your old sitters today," I told her. "I thought you quit playing jokes on people."

"I tried. I really tried. And then I went to some movies on Saturday. And, I don't know. I have all these great jokes. You haven't even seen them all yet — "

"And I don't care to see any more."

Betsy didn't answer that. She was laughing again.

I got up in a huff, opened cupboards until I found the Sobaks' glasses, and poured the rest of my juice into a regular glass. Of course, I picked the fake ice cube out first.

Betsy set it on the table between us. "Isn't it lifelike?" she asked me. She sounded as if she were quoting from an ad.

"Very," I replied. "Where'd you get it?"

"From McBuzz's Mail Order. It's a catalogue. All McBuzz's sells is practical jokes. I spend most of my allowance on stuff from McBuzz's. . . . Well, I used to. Then Mom and Dad made me quit. But it didn't matter. I already had McBuzz's best jokes."

"Oh, good," I said. "You wouldn't want to miss out on a single instrument of torture."

"Want to see a catalogue?" asked Betsy. Before I could answer, she'd dashed out of the kitchen and upstairs. She returned carrying McBuzz's Mail Order.

"Look. Look at the front cover," she instructed me. "This catalogue features rubber chickens and plastic ants."

"Great."

Betsy flipped through the pages. I had to admit that some of the stuff — especially the selection of whoopee cushions — was kind of funny. By the time we'd finished, I'd calmed down.

But when Betsy said, "Want some gum?" I was immediately on my guard again.

"Uh, no," I replied.

"Look," said Betsy, "I'm sorry about the juice. I really am. Here." She pulled two pieces of gum out of her pocket. She kept the Wrigley's for herself. She handed me one in a plain white wrapper.

Well, I might not be a good student, but I'm no fool. I know about trick gum. "Thanks," I said drily, "but I prefer Wrigley's. So let's trade."

Betsy frowned. "We-ell . . . all right."

We swapped sticks, I peeled off the Wrigley's wrapper, popped the gum in my mouth, and, "Aughhh! Oh, EW!" I spit the gum out. "It tastes like pepper! That is so hot!" I grabbed for my glass of apple juice and polished it off, but my mouth was still on fire.

Across from me, Betsy was chewing her own

gum happily and was in hysterics again. "Gotcha! I gave you trick gum!" she cried. "I switched wrappers! I *knew* you wouldn't trust me, so I switched wrappers."

"Why should anyone trust you?" I muttered. It was hard to talk.

I had to do something fast. I was losing control of the situation, and a good baby-sitter always stays in charge. I thought quickly. "Let's play outside," I suggested. What could Betsy do to me outside? If she wanted to get any of her tricks, she'd have to go back in the house — and I simply wouldn't let her.

"Could we play on my swing set?" asked Betsy.

"Sure, anything." I fanned my burning mouth with my hands.

"Goody!" said Betsy, jumping up. "Let's go!"

We put on our jackets, and Betsy ran out her back door. I followed her closely. Betsy's swing set was not in her backyard, where I'd thought it would be. It was by the side of the house, near the Sobaks' driveway.

Betsy jumped onto a swing. She sat there and smiled at me. "You take that one," she said, pointing to the second of three swings.

I shrugged. "Okay."

Betsy watched me like a hawk as I sat on

the swing. She was grinning, but after I'd been on the swing for a moment, her smile turned to a frown. What was with her? She was one weird kid. Wait a sec! Maybe she had booby-trapped the swing or something. I wouldn't put it past her. But I inspected the swing, and it looked fine to me — just a little old.

"Come on," I said. "Let's have a swinging contest. Let's see who can swing the highest."

Betsy immediately began pumping her legs up and down. She really wanted to win. Good. At least her mind was off practical jokes.

I pumped, too. Betsy and I swung higher and higher. I remembered when I was Betsy's age and believed that it was possible to swing so high you'd circle right over the top of the — CLUNK!

I heard a funny, metallic noise. And then . . . the bottom dropped out from under me. The chain on the swing had snapped. Oh, lord, I thought.

You know how sometimes you have an idea that something is going to happen before it actually *does* happen? I don't know if you'd call it ESP exactly, but, well, I just *knew*, without knowing how I knew, that I was going to fall and I was going to be hurt badly.

I was terrified. I could feel my heart beating in my throat, as if it had jumped up there in

fear. And before I had time to do a thing —
this was all happening in a split second — I
was flying through the air. I landed on the
driveway — hard — and heard another noise.
An awful one. It was a crunch. But the odd
thing was, I didn't feel any pain. My leg felt
strange, but it didn't hurt. Still, I knew what
had happened. . . .

"Betsy," I said weakly, trying to sit up. "I
think my leg is broken."

CHAPTER 5

My leg certainly was broken. It was a truly disgusting sight. There was no blood or anything, but it was twisted in a way that no leg should ever *be* twisted. I thought I'd seen all possible disgusting sights from eating school lunches with Kristy Thomas. But this was much, much worse. I had to look away from my leg.

I turned toward Betsy. She was still swinging, but the expression on her face was one of horror. Then, in a panic, she began to slow herself down. The swing hadn't even come to a stop when she jumped off it and ran to me.

"Oh! Oh, Claudia!" she exclaimed. "I'm sorry I'm sorry I'm sorry! I knew the chain was broken. That's why I wanted you to sit down on the swing. I thought when you did, you'd just go — boom — onto the grass. But it didn't break right away and I forgot and you said let's have a contest and I still forgot and I didn't remember until — "

"Betsy, Betsy," I interrupted her. I had suddenly realized that my leg was numb. I could hardly feel it, which scared me more than anything. "I know you didn't mean for this to happen. The thing is, I have to get to the hospital. And you're going to have to help me. Can you follow directions?"

"Yes. I'm very good at it," Betsy said seriously. She was kneeling next to me and had taken one of my hands in both of hers. Suddenly she looked angelic.

"All right," I replied. "I need you to do two things. Listen to both of them now, and then go inside and do them."

"Okay." Betsy's voice was trembling and her eyes had filled with tears.

"First, dial nine-one-one on the telephone. When someone answers, explain that I'm your baby-sitter and I broke my leg and we need an ambulance. Be sure to answer all their questions and to give them your address. Then I want you to make another call."

"To your parents?" Betsy asked.

"No, to yours. Try your mom first. If you can't reach her, try your dad. And if you can't reach *him*, I want you to call the Rodowskys. Do you know Jackie Rodowsky?"

Betsy nodded.

"Okay, my friends Dawn and Mallory are sitting for a group of kids at his house this afternoon. If you have to call them, tell one of them to come over here and stay with you till your mom comes home. If you don't know Jackie's number, can you look it up in the phone book? Rodowsky is spelled, um, R, let's see. . . ."

"Don't worry," said Betsy. "I'm a good speller. I'll find it." She ran inside.

I lay on the driveway and began to shiver, even though it wasn't very cold that day. I hoped I wasn't going into shock or something. I tried to remember what us baby-sitters had learned in the first-aid course we'd taken, but it wasn't easy to concentrate.

It didn't matter. Things began to happen quickly. First, Betsy dashed back out of her house. "I made the calls!" she announced breathlessly. "The ambulance is coming and so are Mallory *and* Dawn. I couldn't reach my mom — no one answered — and Dad's line was busy, busy, busy. Here's a pillow and a blanket," she added. "The nine-one-one person said to give them to you." Betsy tried to make me comfortable, which wasn't easy, considering I couldn't move my leg.

Soon after, Mallory and Dawn came zooming

up the Sobaks' driveway on their bicycles, followed by a bunch of kids, also on bicycles. Dawn threw down her bike and ran to me. "We couldn't let you go through this alone," she said breathlessly. Then she told Mallory and the kids to stand in the front yard and wait for the ambulance. When they were gone, she said, "Okay, Claud. Did Betsy call your parents or Mimi?"

I shook my head.

"All right, then I'll go do that."

"Don't call Mimi!" I cried. "She can't drive. She won't be able to do anything and she'll go crazy worrying."

"Then I'll call your parents. Maybe they can beat the ambulance here."

"I doubt it," I said.

"Well, let me find out. I'll be back in just a sec."

Dawn ran inside and I was alone again for a few minutes. Where was that ambulance? My heart was still beating in my throat.

When Dawn returned, she said, "I reached your mom right away and she's going to call your dad. They're going to meet the ambulance at the hospital. So I'll ride with you, and Mallory will stay here with the kids. We left a note for Mrs. Rodowsky. When Mrs. Sobak comes home, Mallory will tell her what happened. . . . What *did* happen, by the way?"

I tried to explain, but I was feeling pretty woozy. I was very relieved to see the ambulance a few minutes later.

Mallory kept the kids out of the way while the ambulance pulled into the Sobaks' drive. Then the attendants jumped out, checked me over, and carefully (but it still hurt) loaded me onto a stretcher and into the ambulance.

"Her parents are going to meet us at the hospital," Dawn told one of the attendants. "I just called her mother. They couldn't get here before you did, but they'll be at the hospital to sign papers, or — or whatever they have to do."

Just before they shut the doors, Betsy's tearful face peered in at me. "I'm sorry," she said again. "I'm really sorry, Claudia. I didn't mean for this to happen."

"I know you didn't," I told her.

And then the driver slammed the door shut.

"Dawn?" I called. "Where's Dawn?"

"I'm right here," she replied. "I'm up front, next to the driver."

The other attendants, a man and a woman, were in the back with me. They were taking my blood pressure and trying to put something on my leg. To hold the bones in place, I guess.

We sped toward the hospital. I was sort of

disappointed that the driver didn't make the siren wail. I guess they only do that for big emergencies — I mean, like for car accidents. I was glad I wasn't a big emergency, but roaring along with the siren blaring would have been exciting.

After awhile, the ambulance came to a stop and the driver got out.

"We're here, Claud," Dawn said.

The back doors were opened and the stretcher was wheeled out. The stretcher is kind of interesting. It's on these collapsible legs. When the attendants had put me in the ambulance, they'd collapsed the legs to make it fit inside. When they took me out, they pulled the legs down again. Then they wheeled me inside the hospital. It was like being on a traveling bed.

"I don't see your parents yet, Claud," Dawn said, "but I'm sure they'll be here any minute now. You know how traffic can be at this time of day."

I nodded. I thought of the last time I was in the hospital — right after Mimi had her stroke — and I began to cry.

"Hey," said Dawn, running along beside me. She found my hand and held it. "Don't worry, Claud. I mean, go ahead and cry. That's okay. But I know everything's going to be all right. I just know it. Why don't I go watch for your parents? I can tell them where you are. Then I'll come find you. Or your mom and dad will, okay?"

"Okay." My leg was beginning to hurt — a lot. I bit my lip.

It seemed as if Dawn was gone forever. Before she came back, a nurse wheeled me away to have my leg X-rayed. That's all I remember clearly. After that, somebody gave me an injection that made me feel very sleepy. I know I closed my eyes and that a lot of time passed, but I didn't feel like I was asleep. Isn't that weird?

When things finally got clear again, I was somewhere else in the hospital, my leg was stretched out in front of me in a big cast, hanging from a metal frame, and Mom, Dad, Janine, and Dawn were all peering at me. I felt like Dorothy in the movie *The Wizard of Oz* when she wakes up back home in Kansas and finds her family and friends around her.

"Hello, Sleeping Beauty," said Dad.

"Was I really asleep?" I asked.

Everyone laughed.

"What's my leg doing up there?" I went on, pointing to it.

More laughter, but it was gentle and friendly.

"It's in traction," Mom told me. "It's — "

"When did you and Dad and Janine get

here?" I interrupted her. "What time is it?" I felt very confused.

"It's only about a quarter of six, honey," Mom told me. "I got here right after the ambulance did. Dad and Janine arrived a little while later. You drifted off while the doctors set your leg, and now you're in your own hospital room. . . . Well, not your *very* own, you've got a roommate, but — "

"Wait a sec!" My thoughts were whirling. "I'm sorry I keep interrupting you," I said, "but why am I in a hospital room? Tell the doctor to give me crutches so I can go home. When Kristy broke her ankle, she got to go right home."

I saw Mom and Dad exchange one of those parent looks. You know, that look that says, "Oops. I think we've got a problem with our child. How should we handle it?"

Mom moved closer to me and smoothed my hair out of my eyes. "Claudia," she said slowly, "you can't go home yet. You're going to be in the hospital for a week. The break was bad. Not critical," she assured me, "but no hairline fracture, either. The doctor wants you in traction for awhile, then in bed at home for a few more days, and then you can go back to school. They're just not taking any chances, that's all."

46

"I don't want to be here for a week!" I said, beginning to cry.

"But think of it," said Dawn. "You get a vacation from school."

"I'm certain you will have a stream of visitors," added Janine. "Perhaps flowers and cards. I wouldn't mind a week of such attention."

A vacation and flowers and visitors sounded nice. But the hospital didn't. I kept thinking of Mimi. When she was first in the hospital, she was hooked up to about a zillion machines. I was afraid to go near her. She looked dead. The doctors didn't know if she would walk or talk again.

"Will I be able to walk again?" I asked tearfully.

"Oh, of course!" said my mother. "Is that what you're worried about? The healing process will take two or three months, but you're going to walk just fine. This is a broken bone and nothing more."

I nodded. But a horrible thought occurred to me then. What if I'd broken my right *arm* instead of my right leg? What if I'd broken it so badly that I couldn't use it again? Couldn't paint or sculpt or draw? Suddenly I was angry. I was angry at Betsy for putting me in such a rotten situation; angry at Kristy for starting the Baby-sitters Club in the first place; angry at myself for going to the Sobaks', even after I'd been warned that Betsy was a practical joker. What was wrong with all of us? Couldn't we see how stupid we were?

I was angry at the whole world.

Baby-sitting seemed like risky business. Maybe, just maybe, baby-sitting *was* risky business. Maybe I shouldn't do it anymore.

"I'm tired," I told Dawn and my family. "I think I'll go back to sleep."

I wasn't sleepy at all, but I closed my eyes and left them closed until I thought I'd heard everyone leave the room. I wanted to be alone for awhile.

CHAPTER 6

"More flowers!" announced a nurse. "I'll just add them to the collection."

"Maybe we should donate some of your flowers to the nursing home," commented my mother. "I bet they'd appreciate them."

"Claudee, can I make your bed go up and down?" asked Jamie Newton.

"Where's the lunch cart?" Kristy wondered. "I bet hospital food is even grosser than cafeteria food."

It was Saturday. I'd been dreading Saturday. I'd thought that spending a gorgeous weekend cooped up in a hospital room would be as bad as taking a math test. But I was actually having fun — when I wasn't thinking about my baby-sitting accident.

The rules about visitors at Stoneybrook's hospital are pretty relaxed. In fact, there aren't any rules (unless you're in intensive care). Anyone can come visit. And you can have as many visitors at a time as you want, as long as they don't disturb the other patients.

As Janine had predicted, ever since I'd been in the hospital, I really *had* had a stream of visitors. Mimi was usually with me during school hours, but after school and in the evenings — oh, lord! All the members of the club had come by, and so had Mrs. Perkins and Myriah, Mrs. Newton and Jamie (Jamie is four and one of my favorite sitting charges; today was his second visit), Charlotte Johanssen and her mother, Dr. Johanssen (actually, she happened to be on duty in the hospital), Charlotte's dad, my parents and Janine (of course), and even two of my teachers! Boy, was I embarrassed when my teachers came by. I mean, you don't expect teachers to see you in your nightgown. But we actually had a nice visit. They didn't even mention homework. Or my nightgown.

Then there were the flowers. Everyone sent them. I felt so special. My relatives sent them, our neighbors sent them, and Stacey and her parents sent a bouquet from New York. Plus, Stacey had called every day. (Stacey has diabetes and she's been in the hospital quite a few times, so we could swap hospital stories.)

Now it was almost lunchtime on Saturday, and crowded into my half of the room were

Kristy, Jamie, my mother (she'd brought Jamie and Kristy with her), Mr. Pike, Mallory, and two of Mallory's sisters — Vanessa and Claire, who are nine and five.

I felt kind of bad for my roommate, Cathy, who had no visitors, but I knew why she had no visitors. Cathy was (I'm sorry, but this is the truth) a great big baby. She was fourteen, and she'd broken her elbow and had an operation on it. I guess it was a bad break, but every time a doctor or a nurse wanted to do *any*thing to her, she'd scream and cry as if she were two years old. No one knew what to do about it. Her parents tried to spend time with her, but they couldn't be at the hospital every second, and no friends came or called or sent flowers. I decided that this was because Cathy didn't have any friends. *I* wouldn't want to be friends with such a baby. Still, I felt bad for Cathy.

"Mom?" I said as the nurse set the new bouquet of flowers on the windowsill. "Come here for a sec."

Mom had been talking to Mr. Pike and Mallory. She left them and came over to my bed. "What is it, sweetie?"

"Giving some of the flowers to the nursing home is a great idea," I whispered, "but maybe we should give some to Cathy, too. Do you

51

think she would feel insulted? I mean, it's kind of like saying, 'You poor kid, you don't have any flowers at all. I'm so popular I've got more than I can handle. Here, take some of mine.' "

Mom looked thoughtfully at Cathy's side of the room. Our beds were separated by a curtain, but there was hardly any privacy. My side was overflowing with flowers and get-well cards and presents and people. Cathy's side was empty, except for Cathy and her bed.

"Why don't you ask her?" said Mom. "She can hardly get mad with all these people around." Mom grinned slyly.

Usually, I think my parents are dorks, but every now and then they come through.

I grinned back. "First, I better see who the flowers are from," I said. I was keeping a list so I could write thank-you notes. I *hate* writing letters, but I thought that after I'd been in bed long enough, even writing letters wouldn't be boring. Besides, I really appreciated what everyone was doing, and I wanted to let them know it.

I reached for the card that was stuck in the bouquet.

"From Buddy, Suzi, and Marnie," I read out loud. "Get well soon."

"Is that the Barretts?" asked my mother.

I nodded. Our club sits for the Barretts a lot.

"You must be pretty popular with your clients," commented Mom, shaking her head. "I've never seen anything like this."

At the mention of "clients," I felt a funny, crawling sensation ripple through my body, but I shook it off. "Hey, Cathy!" I called.

"Yeah?" Cathy drew our curtain back.

"Would you like these flowers?" I asked her. "I thought they'd look really nice by your bed."

"Well . . . well, sure!" Cathy smiled at me.

Mom set the flowers on Cathy's night table. Then she turned to me. "Honey, Mr. Pike and I are going to go get a cup of coffee. We'll be back in a little while."

"Okay," I replied.

As soon as the adults were gone, I looked at Kristy and Mallory. "All right!" I said. "On our own!"

"And just in time for lunch," added Kristy, as a nurse came in with covered trays for Cathy and me. She set mine on this table that rolls over the bed, right across your lap. Then she raised my bed so I was sitting up higher.

"Cool!" cried Vanessa, watching with interest, at the same time that Jamie said, "*I* wanted to make her bed go up!"

"You can put it down for me after lunch," I told Jamie. "How's that?"

"Okay." Jamie looked satisfied.

"Mallory, I'm hungry," complained Claire. "I want a lunch, too."

"We'll get lunch at home when Daddy comes back," Mal told her.

"You might get to eat something before that, though," I said. I was looking disgustedly at my tray. It held a pale piece of baked chicken, a helping of extremely limp broccoli, something white that I couldn't even identify, a pudding cup, a roll, and a container of milk. "Here, have my pudding," I said to Claire, holding out the container along with a plastic spoon.

Kristy was staring at my tray, bug-eyed. "Well, it's finally happened," she said. "We've found something worse than cafeteria food and airplane food put together."

"I know," I moaned. "What I wouldn't give for a Ring Ding or a big bag of Fritos right now." I thought longingly of the junk-food stash in my room. Since I knew the Baby-sitters Club meetings were being held in my room without me (they had to be, because people call my phone number), I said, "Puh-*lease* sneak some decent food in here next time one of you visits, okay? Look in my desk drawer or under my bed or in almost any shoebox."

Kristy and Mallory agreed, and I tried to eat my lunch.

"Hi, Claud!" someone called from the doorway.

I looked up. There was Mary Anne. She was holding a cardboard carton and looking sort of, oh, furtive. (That's a word Janine uses. It means secretive.) She tiptoed into the room, not saying a word to anyone. Then she smiled at Cathy, said, "Excuse me," pulled the curtain between my bed and Cathy's, and opened the box.

Inside was her kitten, Tigger. "Mew," he said in his tiny voice.

Now, the hospital may not have many rules, but I *know* animals are not allowed.

"I know it, too," Mary Anne said when I mentioned that to her. "But I thought you could use a cuddly visitor."

Everyone crowded around my bed. I pushed my lunch table away and we began cooing over Tigger. I hoped Cathy wouldn't blab, and decided she wouldn't, since I'd just given her flowers.

After a few minutes, Mallory said, "Hey, where's Jamie?"

He was gone.

That caused some panic, as you can imagine.

My friends went to look for him, leaving *me* with Tigger. Thanks a lot. What if a nurse came in? But Jamie was found pretty quickly. He was down the hall, in a room where a little boy was recovering from having his appendix removed.

"What were you doing there?" I asked Jamie.

"Visiting," he answered. "I'm a visitor, right?"

I smiled at him. "Right."

My mom and Mr. Pike returned then, and Mary Anne quickly put Tigger in his box and shoved the box under the bed. Since it was lunchtime, everyone left, except for Mary Anne and Tigger.

The afternoon passed quickly. Dawn arrived, then left later with Mary Anne. (I have to admit, I breathed a sigh of relief to see Tigger go, cute as he was.) Jessi and her sister arrived. They brought me a sock to put over the foot of my cast. The sock looked like a moose head. Once it was on, Becca started laughing and couldn't stop. Cathy laughed, too.

Jessi and Becca left. Ashley arrived. Ashley left.

Then the room was silent. It would be a good time to — *Ring, ring.*

I reached for the phone. Since I'd been in the hospital, every single call had been for me. Not one for Cathy.

"Hello?" I said.

"Hi, Claud! It's me!"

"Stacey! Hello!"

"How are you doing?"

I paused.

Stacey could tell immediately that something was wrong. "How are you *really* doing?" she corrected herself.

"I'm — My leg is okay. It hurts, of course, and being in traction is uncomfortable. And I'd give *any*thing for a Ring Ding, but . . ."

"What's wrong?"

"I've been doing a lot of thinking," I told her. "I keep coming back to this one thing. What if I'd ruined my hands or arms when I fell? Baby-sitting can be dangerous, Stace. And there's a good chance that when I grow up I'll be an artist, not a sitter. I don't want to lose that chance. So I'm thinking of dropping out of the Baby-sitters Club. Just to be on the safe side."

CHAPTER 7

Sunday

Mary Anne, didn't you think the comedy film festival was fun at the time?

"At the time" are the key words, Jessi. Then I did. Now I don't.

I guess it did cause a little trouble.

A little trouble! It landed Claudia in the hospital. And it gave the Pike kids too many ideas.

I'll say. No offense, Mal, but I wish you hadn't had that other sitting job today. Then you would have been helping to sit for your brothers and sisters.

Yeah. Wait'll you hear what they did -- one joke after another.

The triplets don't get McBuzz's Mail Order, do they?

58

I was lying in bed, laughing. Kristy had brought the club notebook by for me to read. I had never had so much fun with it as when I read Jessi and Mary Anne's entry. I'm sure not everything that had happened that afternoon seemed funny then, but it seemed pretty funny later.

The afternoon began when Jessi and Mary Anne arrived at the Pikes', rang their bell, and were frightened out of their wits by seven-year-old Margo, who sprang from behind some bushes, shouting, "BOO!"

"Aughh!" screeched Jessi and Mary Anne.

"Scared you! Scared you!" Margo cried delightedly.

She let her sitters inside the house.

"Hi!" cried Nicky. (Nicky is eight.) "Hi, you guys! Boy, am I glad you're here!"

He stuck out his hand and Mary Anne reached for it. She was thinking, Nicky isn't usually this enthusiastic or this polite, but what the heck.

She shook Nicky's hand.

BZZZZZZ!

"Aughh!" Mary Anne screamed again.

"What is going on out there?" called Mallory.

She rushed into the hallway, followed by her parents.

Nicky was laughing and jumping up and down. "I got Mary Anne with the joy buzzer!" he exclaimed.

"And I scared Mary Anne *and* Jessi!" cried Margo.

Mr. and Mrs. Pike shook their heads.

"Please don't give your sitters a hard time," said Mr. Pike.

"Who, us?" asked Nicky innocently.

"Any of you," their father replied sternly.

Mrs. Pike gave Jessi and Mary Anne some instructions about the afternoon.

"The triplets are out in back," she began. (The triplets are Byron, Adam, and Jordan, and they're ten.) "Vanessa is over at the Braddocks' playing with Haley. And, let's see. Who are we missing? Oh, yes. Claire. She's up in her room, I think.

"All the kids have had lunch," Mrs. Pike went on, "and we'll be back around five-thirty, so you don't have to worry about dinner. Mr. Pike and I will be visiting friends in Haddonfield. Their number is by the phone in the kitchen. I guess that's it. You girls know everything else."

"And I'll be sitting for Jamie Newton, if you need me," added Mal. She checked her watch. "Wow, I better go. See you later. 'Bye, Mom! 'Bye, Dad! 'Bye, you guys!"

Mallory took off on her bike. Her parents took off in their car.

"I think I'll go upstairs and see what Claire is up to," said Jessi.

But before she had moved an inch, the phone rang.

"I'll get it!" said Mary Anne. She answered it in the kitchen. "Hello, Pike residence."

"Hello," said a familiar voice, "is your refrigerator running?"

"*Yes*," said Mary Anne impatiently. That was the oldest goof call in history. She waited for the caller to say, "Then you better go catch it."

"Just checking!" said the voice. The caller hung up.

So did Mary Anne. "Goof call," she said disgustedly to Jessi.

Jessi smiled.

The phone rang again.

"*I'll* get it this time," said Jessi. "Hello?"

"Hello, is Rita Book there?" The caller dissolved into giggles and had to hang up the phone.

Mary Anne and Jessi waited for the phone to ring a third time. When it didn't, Jessi finally headed upstairs, while Mary Anne took Nicky and Margo outside. Jessi found the door to Claire and Margo's room closed.

She knocked on it.

"Come in!" called Claire.

Jessi opened the door — and was hit in the face with a stream of water from Claire's squirt gun.

"Hee, hee, hee!" giggled Claire.

"Boy, you and your brothers and sisters sure are full of tricks," said Jessi, wiping the water out of her eyes.

"We've got some great ones, all right," agreed Claire. "My brothers even have a rubber spider. It's big and yucky and ooky."

Jessi didn't answer her at first. Her eyes had seen something lurking in a corner of the room. She swallowed. "Your brothers?" she repeated. "Are you sure they have the only one?"

"Sure, I'm sure," replied Claire. "And they won't let us girls borrow it."

"Well," said Jessi, backing toward the doorway, "then what is *that*?" She pointed to the corner of the room.

"What?" asked Claire. Then she saw it. "Aughh!" she cried.

Jessi panicked and ran into the hallway. She pulled Claire after her, slamming the door shut. "Oh. Oh, my gosh," she said, panting. "That is the biggest spider I have ever seen. It's as big as a dog! I better get Mary Anne."

Claire began to giggle again. "As big as a dog!" She laughed and laughed.

"It wasn't *that* funny," exclaimed Jessi.

"Yes, it was!" Gasping and giggling, Claire opened the door to the bedroom. She ran to the corner and picked up the spider. "This is the *rubber* one!" she cried. "Fooled you! Fooled you!"

Meanwhile, Mary Anne was outside with the other kids. The triplets were practicing soccer moves, and Nicky and Margo were playing volleyball. All the kids were hot and sweaty, so when Byron asked, "Mary Anne, can we have some ice cream?" Mary Anne said yes.

She brought the kids inside and called Claire and Jessi downstairs.

"Let's make chocolate sundaes," said Byron. "Adam and Jordan and I will make them for everyone, even you and Jessi," he told Mary Anne. "Now you guys just sit down and relax."

Jessi sat down, but Mary Anne said, "Be back in a minute." She headed for the bathroom.

She hadn't been gone long when Jessi heard a cry of, "Oh, dis*gust!*"

Nicky tried hard not to laugh.

Jessi glanced at him suspiciously, then dashed for the bathroom. "What is it?" she called.

"That," Mary Anne replied, pointing to the floor. "It took me a minute before I realized it's *fake* barf."

Jessi looked at the realistic puddle on the floor. "Ew," she said. "Boy, you know what? So far, Margo has scared us, Nicky has joy-buzzed you and left this barf here, Claire has gotten me with a squirt gun and frightened me with a fake spider — "

"And Vanessa goof-called us twice. I'm sure it was Vanessa," Mary Anne finished up. "Listen, we've got to put an end to this, and I think I know how to do it. While we're eating our ice cream," she said, lowering her voice, "I'm going to tell the kids the circus is coming. Just go along with anything I say, okay?"

"Okay," agreed Jessi, mystified.

Mary Anne explained the rest of her idea. Then she picked up the plastic barf and brought it into the kitchen. "Very funny," she said, handing it to Nicky.

Nicky smirked.

"Ice cream's ready!" announced Byron.

Mary Anne, Jessi, Nicky, Margo, and Claire sat down at the Pikes' kitchen table. The triplets served each of them a dish of vanilla ice cream covered with chocolate sauce. Then they carried their own ice cream to the table.

"Oh, boy!" exclaimed Nicky. He dug his

spoon into his dish — and the scoop of ice cream slurped out and bounced across the table.

The triplets laughed until they were almost crying.

"It's a chocolate-covered tennis ball!" Jordan managed to gasp out.

Nicky pouted, but there wasn't much he could say after the joy buzzer and the plastic barf. He just made himself a real sundae.

"So," said Mary Anne, "did you guys hear about the circus? It's coming to town tomorrow. Well, actually, it's coming today, but the first show will be tomorrow. Clive Baity's Traveling Circus, it's called."

The Pikes were intrigued. They wanted to know all about the circus. Mary Anne answered their questions. Practical jokes seemed to have been forgotten. But not for long. When Jessi stood up for a moment to grab a dish towel from the counter, Nicky pulled her chair out from under her, which made her sit down on the floor.

"That does it," Mary Anne whispered to Jessi as she helped her to her feet. "Come in the living room with me. It's time to put our plan into action."

Jessi and Mary Anne sauntered casually into the Pikes' living room. They left the kids in the kitchen, cleaning up the ice cream dishes.

"Oh, my lord!" Mary Anne suddenly screeched. "Jessi, I don't believe it! There is an *elephant* in the front yard!"

"An elephant?" cried Claire from the kitchen.

"Don't listen to her," Adam said. "It's a joke."

Jessi and Mary Anne pretended not to have heard him.

"What's that thing on the elephant's back?" asked Jessi.

"It's — it's a blanket. Why, it says *Clive Baity* on it."

"Oh, no! The elephant must have escaped from the circus! Honest, Mary Anne, I have never, and I mean, *never* seen anything like this in my *whole life!*"

That was enough for the Pikes. Both Jessi and Mary Anne sounded truly stunned. And their story was believable . . . sort of. Besides, baby-sitters don't play tricks, do they?

The Pike kids rushed to the living-room window.

"Where is it?" asked Adam breathlessly.

"Fooled you!" cried Mary Anne.

"And," added Jessi, "this is the *end* of all practical jokes for the day."

Red-faced, the triplets, Nicky, Margo, and Claire went outdoors to play.

And that *was* the last trick of the day — except for when the phone rang, and an odd-sounding voice on the other end said, "Helloo, this is Queen Elizabeth. Is Prince Charles there?"

"Yes, he is," said Jessi, "but he can't come to the phone. He's outside waxing his yacht. Good-bye."

Clunk.

CHAPTER 8

I couldn't believe it. I was going home at last! The week was over. The night before, the doctor had taken my leg out of traction. I still had to stay off my feet for another week, but I would much rather have done that at home than in the hospital.

I was tired of the hospital. My flowers were drooping, I hated the meals (Dawn had saved my life, though, by bringing me some junk food), and I wanted to sleep in my own bed again. Cathy had gone home, and a seven-year-old girl had taken her place. She slept all the time and everyone had to whisper when they came in our room.

The doctor let me go home really, really early one morning. Dad picked me up at seven-thirty. (My parents were trying not to miss too much work.) A nurse pushed me outside in a wheelchair, and she and Dad loaded my stuff into our car. Since I was still in my nightgown and bathrobe, this was fairly embarrassing.

I got over it, though. As Dad drove me through Stoneybrook, I felt as if I'd been let out of prison.

"Boy, am I glad to be going home!" I exclaimed.

"No! Really?" teased my father. "You mean you didn't want a few extra vacation days in the hospital? I'm sure Mom and I could have arranged something."

I laughed. "I won't even mind finishing my thank-you notes, or starting all the homework I'll have to make up."

"Well, we sure are glad to have you back."

"Thanks, Dad."

I thought Mom would already have left for work and Janine for school, but when Dad steered our car into the driveway, there were Mom, Janine, Mimi — and Mary Anne! They were crowded onto our front porch, and they waved madly when they saw the car.

I rolled my window down. "Hi!" I called.

"Welcome home!" they replied.

I've never had so much help in my life. Everyone rushed to the car. Janine opened my door. Mom and Mary Anne tried to get me out. Dad rushed around to give them a hand.

Mimi opened another door and began pulling my things out of the car.

At last I was inside and settled on the couch in the den.

"This is where you can stay, for the most part," said Mom. "You'll be downstairs with Mimi, and you've got the television and a phone, even if it isn't *your* phone. At night, you can go up to your room."

"For club meetings, too," Mary Anne added. She looked at her watch. "Gosh, I better go. I'll be late. . . . Uh, stay right by the phone for a while, Claud. Okay?"

"Why?" I asked. (As if I could go anywhere anyway.)

"Never mind," Mary Anne replied. She dashed off for school.

"I'm afraid I've got to leave now, too, honey," said my mother.

"So do I," said Dad and Janine at the same time. Before they left, Mom and Dad hugged me, and Janine gave me a stack of magazines to read. She had bought them especially for me. I knew this because the only magazines Janine reads have names like *The Joy of Physics* or *Science, Technology, and You*. What she had given me were *People, Tiger Beat, Seventeen,* and *Vogue*.

"Boy! Thanks!" I said enthusiastically.

My family left in a rush. Mimi and I were alone together. We looked at each other happily.

"I hope I'm not going to be too much work for you," I said. "I don't want to tire you out."

"You not work at all!" Mimi exclaimed. "We have nice week. I know."

"I can get to the bathroom myself," I assured Mimi. "Dad left my crutches right there on the floor. And last night, I practiced on them after they took my leg out of traction."

"Yes, fine," said Mimi approvingly. "Oh. I have pre — pre — gift for you. A moment. I be back."

Mimi left the den. She returned with a paper bag in her hands. "Here," she said. "Open."

I peeked inside the bag. Then I let out a screech. "Oh, thank you! A Nancy Drew book! That's great! I haven't read this one. Mimi, you're the best."

Mimi smiled. "Now, my Claudia," she said, "I fix breakfast. You did not have breakfast at the hospital?"

"No," I told her. "I left too early. Oh boy, Mimi. One of your breakfasts would be great. At the hospital, all they had was, like, Wonder Bread and runny eggs. They couldn't even make good tea. It was weak and pale. So I'm dying for one of your breakfasts. And I'm starving."

Mimi left for the kitchen. I lay back against my pillows. I had noticed something during the past week. Any time I was alone — when there were no doctors or nurses or visitors around me — thoughts about baby-sitting crept into my head. I had a huge problem, and I had no idea what to do about it. The thing was, I love being a member of the Baby-sitters Club. My friends might not realize that, since art is so important to me, too, and Ashley once almost talked me into quitting the club so I could spend more time on my art. But the club is a big part of my life. I knew that. So I didn't want to drop out of it at all.

On the other hand, the thought of baby-sitting terrified me now. Suddenly it seemed like too many things could go wrong. And if I was afraid to sit — how could I be part of the club?

Ring, ring!

The phone! Mary Anne had said to stay by it. I answered it excitedly.

"Hello?"

"Hello," said a man's voice. "Is this Claudia?"

I recognized the voice. It belonged to my homeroom teacher.

72

"Hi!" I said.

"Hi, there. This is your whole homeroom. I've got you on a speaker phone so everyone can hear you."

"Oh!" I exclaimed. "Hi, you guys!"

My teacher must have aimed the receiver out at the class then, because suddenly I heard twenty-one voices say, "Welcome home, Claudia!"

"Thanks," I replied.

Then I got to say hi to every single kid in the class, individually. I didn't talk to most of them very long, but when Kristy got on, we had a discussion about my homework.

"I'll collect it for you, if you want," she said, "and give it to you at our meetings. On Tuesday and Thursday, I'll send it home with Mary Anne."

"Hey, how did Mary Anne know about this phone call?" I asked.

"Oh, we've had it planned forever. We were hoping you'd come home on a weekday. We were dying to do this."

"I'm glad you did," I said. "It's too bad Mary Anne isn't in our homeroom."

"Oh, I gotta go, Claud," said Kristy suddenly. " 'Bye!"

Someone else picked up the phone. "Claudia?" said my teacher again. "The bell is about to ring, so we'll have to hang up."

"Thank you for calling," I told the class. "I really appreciated it."

"Good-bye!" shouted the kids.

I could hear the bell ring then, so I got off the phone. Just as I was hanging up, Mimi came into the den, carrying a tray.

"Oh, goody. Breakfast," I said.

"Who was on phone?" Mimi asked.

I told her about the call as she handed me the tray. "Oh, Mimi. This looks super!" I exclaimed.

On the tray were waffles and bacon, orange juice and tea. Strong tea. Mimi had even put a flower in a bud vase.

Mimi sat at the end of the couch and watched me eat.

"You know what?" I said to her, my mouth full of bacon.

"What, my Claudia?"

"The doctor says I'll have to have physical therapy after he takes the cast off. Exercises and stuff."

"I am sure you do them fine," Mimi said. "Practice, practice."

"It'll probably hurt."

"A little. Will hurt a little, yes. But you will do it."

"Mimi? Were you ever scared after you had your stroke?"

"Oh, plenty. Very scared."

"You know what I'm scared of?" I said. "I'm scared to baby-sit again."

Mimi looked thoughtful. "What is really scary," she told me, "is to think we do not have control. Cannot keep accident from happening. Or stroke from happening."

"Well, I know one way to have a little control. I won't baby-sit. Then I won't be exposed to kids and their toys and tricks."

"Is that what really want?" asked Mimi.

I shook my head. "I don't know."

"You must think over," said Mimi solemnly. "Very important. You have any ideas, you need any help, you come to me, my Claudia."

"I know. I know I can do that. Thanks."

When I had cleaned my plate, Mimi took the tray away. She returned a little later with a cup of tea for herself.

Mimi looked at her watch. "Oh! Claudia! I put on TV. Time for *Wheel of Fortune!*"

I'd forgotten about Mimi and *Wheel of Fortune.* She'd started watching the daytime reruns of the show last summer when she was recovering from her stroke. I'd thought they might be helpful. (The word games improved her reading and vocabulary.) Mimi had gotten hooked.

She switched on the TV and we settled into the show.

"Spin wheel! Spin wheel!" Mimi would cry. "No, don't guess *now!*"

Mimi and I played along. If we had been contestants, we would have won a lot of prizes. Well, a few anyway. Oh, all right, *Mimi* would have won prizes. Then we watched *Gilligan's Island* and *I Love Lucy*. I read my Nancy Drew for awhile. After lunch, Mimi and I watched soap operas.

If I could just forget about the baby-sitting problem, I thought, having a broken leg wouldn't be bad at all.

CHAPTER 9

My cast was a work of art. No kidding. Now that I was out of traction and could reach it, I couldn't keep my hands (or my Magic Markers) off of it. It was just too tempting a drawing surface. I know you're supposed to let your friends sign your cast — and I was going to do that — but those big white spaces seemed to me to be jumping up and down, screaming, "Color me! Color me!" Huge areas of my cast were solidly covered with designs and sketches.

On the day of the first club meeting after I came back from the hospital, I lounged on my bed, waiting for my friends and illustrating my cast. A few minutes before, Mimi had watched me climb the stairs to my room. She wouldn't let me do it with the crutches unless someone else came with me (she thought it was dangerous), so I had figured out a way to back up the stairs on my bottom. It looked really stupid, but it was safe.

Downstairs, I heard the front door open and a squeal as someone (probably Mary Anne) greeted Mimi. Then I heard footsteps on the stairs and finally Mary Anne appeared.

"Hi!" I greeted her. "I thought it was you."

"Hi! . . . Can I sign your cast?"

"Sure."

"Oh, goody. I've got a really cute autograph."

Mary Anne took one of my pens and carefully wrote:

I 🚗 cry,
I 🚗 laugh,
to think you want
my 🚗 - graph!

While she was working on that, the rest of the club members arrived. Jessi was the last one, as usual. She has a busy schedule in the afternoons, and she dashed in just as Mary Anne capped her pen, and Kristy said, "This meeting will now come to order. I move that we all sign Claudia's cast and welcome her back."

Everyone dove for my Magic Markers (except Mary Anne).

"Mary Anne," I said, "I think we could use some refreshments. Look under my bed and see what you can find."

Mary Anne disappeared, then returned triumphantly with one large bag of pretzels and two small bags of M&Ms.

"Kristy, that's mean!" Dawn suddenly exclaimed, leaning over to read what Kristy had written on my cast. "Listen, you guys. It says, 'God made the rivers, God made the lakes, God made Claudia . . . well, we all make mistakes.'"

Jessi and Mal started to giggle. "That's not mean!" said Jessi. "It's funny."

"No, it's mean," cried Dawn, but she was laughing, too.

So were Kristy and a dust-covered Mary Anne.

"Autographs are dumb," Mal announced.

Everyone was talking and laughing and arguing. How could I decide not to be part of such a great group of people? I must be crazy. But I was pretty sure I was going to have to leave the club. I would tell my friends whenever the time seemed right.

"Order, order!" cried Kristy. "This is a meeting, everybody, not a party. Come on. We have business to take care of.''

We settled down. I was stretched out on my bed. Dawn was at my feet, still doodling on my cast. Mary Anne, who usually sits with us on the bed, sat with Mal and Jessi on the floor, since I was taking up so much space. And Kristy, of course, sat in the director's chair, her visor in place. ''Okay, Dawn,'' she said, waving her pen around as she spoke, ''how's the treasury? Are we in good shape?''

''We're fine . . . but Claudia owes dues from when she was in the hospital.''

I blushed. The thing was, I didn't want to pay dues if I was going to drop out of the club.

''Are you broke?'' Dawn asked. ''If you are, don't worry about it. You can make up for it next week.''

''No, it's not that,'' I said uncomfortably. ''It's, um, it's . . .'' I was hoping the phone would ring then and let me off the hook (get it?), but no such luck. ''See, I did a lot of thinking in the hospital,'' I began. ''And, well, you know how important my art is to me. I really want to be an artist when I grow up. Or maybe a clothes designer. So I thought, what if I had broken my arm or smashed my hands when I fell? What if I had hurt myself so badly that I couldn't draw or paint anymore?''

"But you didn't," Mallory pointed out sensibly.

"But I could have," I said.

"What are you getting at?" asked Kristy, with narrowed eyes.

"I'm getting at . . . I . . . I-want-to-drop-out-of-the-club," I said in a rush. "Baby-sitting is too dangerous."

"Claudia!" everyone cried. "You can't do that!"

The phone did ring then, but we didn't all dive for it, like we usually do. Kristy picked it up after glaring at me for a moment and arranged for Dawn to sit for the Perkins girls. Then she turned to me. She looked as if she was about to let her mouth go on a rampage, but Mary Anne jumped in ahead of her.

"Claud," she said, "we understand that you must be scared. Your accident was awful. But it wasn't caused by baby-sitting."

"Of course it was," I told her.

"No. It was caused by Betsy Sobak. And not even on purpose. You know she didn't mean for that to happen."

"It did happen, though."

"Claudia, we don't want to lose you," said Dawn. "Are you absolutely *sure* you want to drop out of the club?"

"No," I told her. "But I'm pretty sure."

"Look," said Kristy, "you can't baby-sit for awhile anyway, can you?"

"Not unless I get a walking cast," I said, "which might happen. But I don't think I'd be much good on crutches."

"All right, then. Instead of dropping out of the club, why don't you see how it feels not to sit for awhile? Maybe you'll miss it a lot."

I thought about that as a few more job calls came in. I passed around the pretzels and M&Ms. I chewed and thought some more.

"Okay," I told the club members at last, "I won't decide right away. But I want you to know that I'm thinking about it."

"That's fair," said Kristy.

"Darn old Betsy Sobak," muttered Dawn. "Look what she's caused."

"You know, I thought I was prepared for anything," I said. "Before the swing broke that afternoon, Betsy had already gotten me with a dribble glass, a fake ice cube with a fly in it, and pepper gum."

"Oh, you were lucky then," said Mallory. "After you guys went to the hospital, *I* got to see Betsy's room. It's, like, a joke warehouse in there. She's got a rubber chicken, glow-in-the-dark lizards, a giant cockroach, plastic ants, a squirting hair ribbon, an exploding cigar, and a fake bloody tooth."

"I suppose we have McBuzz to thank for all of that, whoever McBuzz is," I said.

Mallory nodded.

The phone rang again and Mary Anne picked it up. As she spoke, she kept raising her eyebrows and making faces at us. At last she said to the caller, "I'll get right back to you." She hung up. *"That,"* she told us, "was Mrs. Sobak. She needs another sitter."

"Boy!" I exclaimed. "If I were Mrs. Sobak, I wouldn't have the nerve to call us again. Her daughter nearly killed me."

Dawn rolled her eyes. "She didn't nearly kill you."

"Besides," added Mallory, "when I met Mrs. Sobak, I sort of got the impression that she doesn't think Betsy misbehaves. She just thinks she's kind of . . . well, she called her high-spirited. And I — Oh! Oh, my gosh! Have I ever got an idea!" Mallory suddenly cried. "Kristy, if I'm free, *please* can I take the job with Betsy? See, there's been a lot of practical joking going on in my house — "

"Tell me about it," said Jessi.

"So I know a lot of tricks now myself," Mallory finished up. "And I could borrow some stuff from the triplets."

"You mean, *you'd* play jokes on *Betsy?*" exclaimed Kristy.

Mallory nodded. "Bad idea?"

Kristy frowned. "I don't know about that, Mal. Playing tricks on a little kid. . . . I just don't know. It seems sort of mean. On the other hand . . ." Kristy's voice trailed off and I could tell she was thinking — hard. "You were certainly patient with Betsy, Claud," she said at last.

"Yeah, and look what she did to her," Mallory chimed in.

"I know, I know," said Kristy, and her eyes were beginning to gleam. "Well, maybe that would work. Obviously, we have a problem and we have to do something about it. I suppose we could declare a practical-joke war on Betsy Sobak. An unofficial one, of course. I mean, we can't tell her about it. But maybe it would teach her something. Mary Anne, is Mallory free to take the job?"

Mary Anne checked the appointment calendar in the record book. "Yup," she replied. "I'll call Mrs. Sobak."

Kristy looked at me. "The war is on," she said with a grin.

I felt a lot better.

But after dinner that night, Ashley called, and I made a mistake. I told Ashley I might drop out of the club.

"Good for you!" Ashley declared. "I'm really glad to hear that."

"You are?" I replied.

"Sure. I've always told you: If you want to be a serious, professional artist, you have to devote more time to your art. You can't be baby-sitting every day. Think of the extra classes you could take if you weren't sitting."

I thought about them. I could take water-colors or portrait-painting or still life. But for some reason, that didn't cheer me up. And *that* should have told me something. It didn't, though. Not then. So I let it go by.

At the club meeting, I had bought time. Kristy had pointed out that I couldn't sit for awhile anyway. How would I feel without kids around me? Without jobs? Without a way to earn money? Would I miss Jamie and the Perkins girls and the Pike kids? It would be an interesting test.

Even more interesting, however, would be watching to see who won the practical-joke war.

CHAPTER 10

Thursday

When I went over to Betsy Sobak's, I was armed with a package of sneezing powder, a rubber slug, and a very realistic-looking furry rat. I had rented them from the triplets for the afternoon. It cost me $1.50 -- 50¢ per triplet. Anyway, I was feeling pretty confident when I reached the Sobaks', but I was also jumpy. I knew I would have to be on my toes with Betsy....

Hey, Mallory, remind me at our next meeting that we should pay you back the $1.50 "rental fee" from the treasury.

-- Kristy

The joke war was on, even though us sitters were the only ones who knew it. We had declared it at the last meeting, and we weren't going to stop fighting until we had won it. We'd never had a problem we couldn't handle, and we weren't going to let Betsy get the best of us.

This was the main idea of a speech Kristy gave at the end of the meeting during which we had declared war. Mallory found Kristy's words running through her head as she rode her bike over to Betsy's on Thursday afternoon. She told me later that as she pedaled along, she tried to psych herself up, the way boxers do before important fights. She talked to herself, encouraged herself, reminded herself of the jokes she had rented and that she knew what jokes Betsy kept in her room. By the time she reached the Sobaks', she felt prepared — on guard and ready.

Before Mrs. Sobak left, she told Mallory that Betsy would want a snack first thing, so as soon as Mal and Betsy were on their own, Mal said, "What would you like for a snack, Bets?"

"Cookies," Betsy replied immediately. "Cookies and milk."

"Okay," said Mal. "*I'll* fix the snack." She wasn't taking any chances. "Furthermore,"

Mal added, "you sit right here at the kitchen table while I fix it." Mal was trying to keep Betsy away from her stock of jokes.

"Okay," said Betsy obediently.

Mal stood at the counter, taking cookies from the jar and pouring glasses of milk. Every so often, she looked over her shoulder at Betsy.

Betsy was just sitting in her chair. She was barely moving.

Mallory never let her guard down, though. She carried everything to the table at once, so Betsy couldn't switch anything around or add anything weird to the food — like plastic ants or ice cubes with flies in them.

But Betsy was an absolute angel during the snack.

Maybe she's learned her lesson, thought Mallory.

Betsy bit into a cookie. She chewed it thoughtfully. "How's Claudia?" she asked.

"Not bad, considering," Mallory replied. "She's home from the hospital, which means her leg isn't in traction anymore. But she can't go back to school yet. She might get a walking cast later, but she's not sure."

"What's a walking cast?" Betsy asked politely. (She had a milk mustache.)

"It's a shorter cast and it has this piece on the bottom, sort of like the heel of a shoe, only sturdier, so you can walk around as if you had two regular legs."

"Oh." Betsy nodded solemnly. Then she noticed that Mallory had finished her cookies and milk. "Want some more?" she asked.

"Yes, thanks. Oh, but I'll get it," Mal answered quickly.

She opened the refrigerator and stood in front of it, pouring milk into her glass. She'd been planning on having another cookie, too, but realized that she hadn't been able to keep her eyes on them while she'd had her back turned, so she decided she better not take one after all. They'd probably been coated with itching powder or something by then. Even seeing Betsy take another cookie didn't convince Mal that the rest were safe.

"How was school today?" Mal asked Betsy. (What a dumb question, she thought, but she didn't know Betsy very well. Besides, it might be a dumb question, but it also seemed *safe*.)

"It was fine. Our class is going to be in a school program. We're going to recite *Wynken, Blynken, and Nod*. We're doing choral speaking. Do you know that poem?"

"Parts of it," said Mal.

"It goes like this: Wynken, Blynken, and Nod one night sailed off in a wooden shoe — sailed on a river of crystal light — "

"Into a sea of dew," Mal chimed in.

Then she and Betsy said together, " 'Where are you going and what do you wish?' the old moon asked the three. 'We have come to fish for the herring fish that live in this beautiful sea; nets of silver and gold have we!' Wynken, Blynken, and Nod."

"Hey, you're good!" Betsy said approvingly to Mal. "Did you do choral speaking in third grade, too?"

Mal shook her head. "Nope. I just like poetry. My two other favorite poems are *The Owl and the Pussycat* and *Jabberwocky*."

Betsy and Mal had finished eating by then.

"You like those, too?" asked Betsy. "I read *The Owl and the Pussycat* to myself. Our teacher read *Jabberwocky* to us. Hey, I've got *The Owl and the Pussycat* in the den. Want me to get it?"

"Sure!" said Mallory. She couldn't believe how well things were going. Not only was Betsy on her best behavior, but she shared an interest of Mallory's. Maybe my accident had taught Betsy a lesson, and she'd sworn off practical jokes.

"I'll clean up our snack while you get the book," Mal added.

Betsy ran off. A few seconds later, Mallory heard the doorbell ring.

"I'll get it!" called Betsy.

"Okay," Mal replied. She heard feet running through the hallway, followed by the sound of the front door opening. Then she heard Betsy talking to someone. And then she heard the door close. . . . Silence.

"Betsy!" Mal called.

No answer.

"BETSY!"

No answer.

Now, if Mal were a panicky person, she might have thought Betsy had gone out to play with someone without her permission. But Mallory is sensible. She looked out the window and didn't see Betsy or any other kids. And she hadn't heard a car pull away, so she knew Betsy hadn't gone off with anyone. Betsy must be inside, and she was probably playing another joke.

Mallory threw down the sponge she'd been wiping the table with, and cried, "Betsy Sobak, I know you're hiding! You come out this instant!"

Boy, is Betsy sly. She had lulled Mallory into thinking she was a normal kid, then WHAM! She pulled a stunt when Mallory wasn't prepared.

"Betsy, you're asking for it!" Mallory shouted. She searched the house from top to bottom.

She looked under tables, behind couches, under beds. Then she looked outdoors.

No Betsy.

Finally, Mallory really *did* start to worry. She went back in the house and was passing by a closet, when the door burst open and Betsy jumped out, shouting, "BOO!"

"Betsy!" Mal admonished her.

Betsy burst into giggles. "Gotcha!"

"I checked that closet twice! Were you in there all the time?"

Betsy nodded. "Well, almost all the time. First I rang the bell, then I tiptoed back to the living room and pretended to answer the door. Then I hid. I'll show you how I hid." She ducked into the closet, stepped into a pair of her father's galoshes, then wrapped an overcoat around her. The coat was still on its hanger. Betsy was disguised as raingear. She was nearly invisible.

Mallory had to admit that the prank was original, but she was mad at Betsy for making her worry. However, she didn't want to give Betsy the satisfaction of *seeing* that she was mad. Instead, she said, "Okay. Very funny. Come on out now. Oh, and if you do, I'll show you this new powder I got yesterday."

That brought Betsy out in a hurry. Mal knows

that most girls Betsy's age like powder and perfume and makeup. Her sister Vanessa does. Mal opened her purse. She took out the sneezing powder. It was in a fancy little jar. "Here," she said, and poured a small amount into Betsy's hands.

Betsy rubbed her hands together, then sniffed them, and . . . "ACHOO!"

"Bless you," said Mallory politely.

"Ah-ah-CHOO! ACHOO! . . . *ACHOO!*"

Betsy began sneezing and laughing at the same time. "Is this sneezing — ACHOO! — powder?" she managed to ask.

"Yup!" (Mal was quite proud of herself.)

"Oh, great joke. I knew that powder was going to be fake. I better — ACHOO! — get a Kleenex."

Betsy ran off and returned with a tissue. "Ah-ah-ACHOO-*OO!* . . . Oh, no!" Betsy cried. She was holding something in her hand. "I sneezed my tooth out!" she exclaimed.

Mallory was worried, until she realized it was the fake bloody tooth she had seen in Betsy's room. She narrowed her eyes. Time to get even . . . again.

During the rest of the afternoon, Mal scared Betsy with the slug, Betsy scared Mal with a rubber snake. Mal scared Betsy with the rat,

Betsy scared Mal with her cockroach. Just as Mal ran out of jokes, she heard Mrs. Sobak's car pull into the garage.

Betsy and Mal looked at each other. They smiled. Mallory was almost embarrassed to admit it, even to herself, but she and Betsy had actually had fun that afternoon. Well, not when Betsy had hidden from Mal. That wasn't fun. But the other jokes, the harmless ones, were cause for an awful lot of giggling.

And Mal knew something just from looking at Betsy then. She knew that neither of them would mention the jokes to Betsy's mother. As a baby-sitter, Mal shouldn't have been playing them on one of her charges. But *Betsy* shouldn't have been playing jokes after what had happened to me.

A battle of the joke war had been fought, but nobody had won and nobody had lost.

CHAPTER 11

Saturday
        I prepared for my sitting
job with Betsy by calling my
brother in California. When I
explained to Jeff what was going
on, he said, "Boy, Dawn. Awesome!
You could scare her with a
rubber spider! You could pretend
there's a mouse loose in the
house... or a rat! Or you could
pretend to faint, and then when
she bends over to see how you
are, jump up and scare her.
Oh, and you could stuff her
room with wadded-up news-
paper so she can't get inside!"
        Well, some of Jeff's ideas were
good. I went to the Sobaks'
well-armed....
        Hey, Dawn, remind me at our next
meeting that we should pay you back for
the call to California.
                                —Kristy

95

Dawn left for Betsy's house feeling less confident than Mallory had. She was prepared with some tricks, but by then she knew that Betsy hadn't given up her practical joking, no matter what Mrs. Sobak said or thought.

Dawn was carrying a rubber spider with her. It wasn't the triplets', since she didn't want to have to rent anything. She knew it was probably too tame a trick for Betsy. (After all, Betsy had all sorts of rubber things of her own.) But Dawn thought the spider was worth a try. Under the right circumstances, anything could be scary. Dawn had borrowed the spider from Buddy Barrett.

Also, she had polished up her acting skills. (Did she even *have* any acting skills to polish up? she wondered.) She was prepared to scream and jump up and down as if she had seen a mouse, she was prepared to pretend to faint, and she was prepared to be very dramatic about both things.

Last but not least, Dawn had brought her Kid-Kit with her. She was hoping that maybe a good distraction was all Betsy needed.

Dawn was sitting for Betsy on a Saturday, from ten o'clock until three o'clock, while her parents went to a golf tournament. She was relieved that she didn't have to feed Betsy first thing. I had had to, and Mallory had had to, and each time the snack had somehow led to a major joke. But by the time Dawn arrived, Betsy had already eaten breakfast and Mrs. Sobak said Dawn didn't have to make lunch until about twelve-thirty.

As soon as the Sobaks had left, Dawn said to Betsy, "Want to see the Kid-Kit I brought with me?"

"What's a Kid-Kit?" asked Betsy suspiciously.

Ah-*ha!* thought Dawn. Betsy is suspicious. That must mean that she's worried about having jokes played on *her.* Well, she had every reason to be suspicious.

"A Kid-Kit," said Dawn, "is just a box full of fun. Toys and games and stuff. I left it in the living room. Come on and take a look at it."

Dawn led Betsy into the living room. They sat on the floor with the Kid-Kit between them.

"I brought Old Maid," Dawn began as she opened the box, "and Mad Libs and a really great book called *Mrs. Piggle-Wiggle* and some other stuff."

Dawn was looking at Betsy as she spoke, but fishing around in the Kid-Kit with one hand. She felt the deck of cards, she felt some books, she felt a pad of paper and a box of crayons, she felt slime. . . .

"Aughh! Oh, no! Ew!" Dawn jerked her hand out of the Kid-Kit. "Oh, there's something slimy in there!" She looked at her hand. "And it's green . . . and it's *on me!* Ew! GROSS!"

Dawn was just working up the nerve to look inside the Kid-Kit when she realized that Betsy's face was turning red.

"Betsy," said Dawn warningly.

Betsy burst out laughing. "Gotcha! I slimed you!" she cried. "I slimed you! I saw the Kid-Kit as soon as you came in. While you were talking to Mom and Daddy, I dumped the slime in the box. And you put your hand right in it!"

"That's nice, Betsy," said Dawn. "That's very nice. Thank you so much. I want you to know that I really appreciate your ruining my Kid-Kit."

"Oh, it's not ruined," Betsy assured her. "The slime is just one big glob. I can get it all out of the box at once. I'll show you."

Betsy reached her hand in the box and withdrew the slime. Sure enough, it was in one big glob. Dawn checked the Kid-Kit anyway, though.

The slime was gone.

"Where do you keep it?" asked Dawn.

"The slime?" said Betsy. "In this can." Betsy pulled a can out from under a chair, where she'd apparently been hiding it. She dropped the slime back in. *Slurp.*

"What a disgusting noise," said Dawn, trying to look ill. "That slime is . . . Oh . . . Oh, my. . . ." Dawn raised her hand to her forehead.

"What's wrong?" asked Betsy, looking alarmed. She put the lid on the can and set the slime on the table.

"I — I feel a little . . . a little . . . faint," Dawn replied weakly. And with that, she flopped over onto the rug.

"Dawn!" Betsy exclaimed. "Dawn, wake up!"

Dawn waited until she was pretty sure Betsy was leaning over her. Then she opened her eyes and shouted, "BOO!"

"Eeee!" cried Betsy, leaping back.

Dawn began to laugh.

After a moment, so did Betsy.

Dawn shrugged her shoulders. There seemed to be no beating the practical-joke queen.

"Come sit on the couch," Betsy said to Dawn. "I'm sorry about the slime." Betsy stood up, sat on the couch, and patted the seat next to her.

An apology. That was a good sign. Maybe Betsy would want to read for awhile. Dawn got *Mrs. Piggle-Wiggle* and joined Betsy.

FWOOOOOO!

Suddenly Betsy was hysterical again. "Gotcha with the pooh-pooh cushion!" she exclaimed.

That did it. Dawn lost no time in pretending she'd seen a mouse. She screamed, "A MOUSE!" and jumped up on a chair. Before she could even think, Betsy did the same thing.

"Got *you!*" cried Dawn. "There is no mouse!"

Once again, Betsy laughed.

Another joke battle was on. Betsy startled Dawn with a fountain pen that squirted water at her. Dawn pulled out the rubber spider. Betsy pulled out a fat rubber toad. That was unfortunate, because by then, Dawn had run out of tricks.

She decided to try reasoning with Betsy. "*Why* do you play jokes all the time?" she asked her.

"Because I like to," Betsy replied.

How could Dawn argue with that? The kid just liked jokes. And she was quick to point out that her baby-sitters played them, too.

"Well, do you think you could stop for awhile?" asked Dawn. "It would be a refreshing change."

So Betsy stopped. She and Dawn played

with some of the stuff in the slime-free Kid-Kit. They actually had a good time. They even got so involved in a game of Monopoly that Dawn forgot about lunch until she heard Betsy's stomach growl. She looked at her watch.

"Quarter of one!" she cried. "Betsy, we've got to eat lunch."

"Aw, but — " Betsy started to protest.

"It's okay," Dawn told her. "We'll leave the game right here. We'll come back to it after lunch."

"Okay," said Betsy.

Dawn fixed soup and sandwiches. After she and Betsy had eaten, Betsy sat back in her chair and looked at Dawn thoughtfully. "I'm really sorry," she said quietly. "You know, about the jokes. All of them." This time Betsy sounded as if she meant it.

"You are?" Dawn replied. "Well, I'm glad to hear you say that. It isn't easy to apologize."

Betsy shook her head. "No, it isn't," she agreed. "And you know what? To make up for what I did, I'm going to fix us a special dessert."

Dawn was about to refuse, since she doesn't eat junk food, but she knew that now was not the time to turn down Betsy's offer. Betsy was trying to make up for things. Wasn't she?

"Okay," said Dawn. "What kind of dessert?"

"Ice-cream sundaes."

Dawn sighed. Not only did she *really* not want any ice cream, but she remembered Mary Anne and Jessi's experience when the triplets had fixed sundaes. However, that was the Pikes' house, not the Sobaks'.

"Great!" said Dawn, hoping she sounded enthusiastic. "I'll clean up the kitchen table, you make the sundaes."

By the time Dawn had put the leftover food away and loaded the dishwasher, Betsy was carrying two dishes to the table. She had made real sundaes — ice cream topped with whipped cream, a cherry, and chopped peanuts. Dawn wished she liked sundaes better.

Betsy set one dish in front of Dawn and sat down with the other. She took a bite. "Oh, heavenly," she said. She closed her eyes for a moment.

Reluctantly, Dawn lifted *her* spoon. She just knew she was going to regret this. She would probably get pimples and cavities from all the sugar. She was concentrating so hard on how unhealthy the ice-cream was that she forgot about who had dished it out — the practical-joke queen. She put the spoon in her mouth. And then she did something she had never done before. Well, at least not since she was

102

a very little kid. She spit her mouthful back out.

"Oh, dis*gus*ting!" she cried. "Betsy, what is this? It tastes like soap."

"It's shaving cream! Gotcha!" Betsy managed to choke out. "I got whipped cream. You got shaving cream!"

Dawn just shook her head.

When Mr. and Mrs. Sobak came home, Dawn didn't say a word about the jokes. She couldn't. It would seem like tattling. And it sounded so babyish.

But babyish or not, another battle in the practical joke war had been fought   and Dawn was pretty sure that this time Betsy Sobak had won.

CHAPTER 12

I was bored.

Not just a little bit, rainy-day sort of bored. I was loll-around-the-house, complain-about-everything bored. I was so bored I *wanted to go back to school.*

It was hard to believe.

I don't know how Mimi put up with me.

It was a Monday afternoon. I'd been home from the hospital since a week before the previous Thursday (longer than the doctor had first said I would have to stay home). The good news was that I didn't have to stay in bed so much and I could go back to school on Wednesday. The bad news was that by that time I would have missed three weeks of school. Even though I'd been keeping up with my homework, I was worried about the classwork I'd missed. When you're me, it's not a good idea to miss three weeks of school. It's hard enough keeping up when you're there every day.

"Mimi," I said, as I waited for my friends to arrive for our club meeting, "what if I have to stay back? Do you think I'll have to repeat eighth grade? It would be horrible! All my friends would go on to the high school and I'd be left behind with a bunch of drippy former seventh-graders who probably wouldn't even — "

"Claudia, my Claudia," Mimi interrupted me.

She was sitting at the kitchen table, shelling peas for dinner. I was supposedly helping her, but I'd reached that point where I was so bored I didn't *want* to do anything.

That doesn't make much sense, does it? You'd think if you were bored enough, you'd be happy for little chores. Like, if someone came up to you and said, "Would you please pick the lint balls off my sweater?" you'd say, "Oh, thank you thank you thank you. Thank you so much for this opportunity. I've been waiting for something like this." But that wasn't the case with me. The boreder I got, the less I wanted to do — except start my regular life again.

"Claudia, you let imani — ima — you let

thoughts run away with you," said Mimi. "No. I think you do not have to repeat grade. You are worry too much. If you fall very far behind, maybe summer school. But your mother, your father, your sister, and I — we help you."

I nodded. "I know you will. I guess I'm just nervous. I've never missed three weeks of school before. At first it did seem like a vacation. Now it doesn't seem like one at all."

"You know, my Claudia," said Mimi gently, and she stopped shelling the peas for a moment, "I have idea about you. I am not . . . I am not . . . head doctor, but this is what I think. I think you worry about school because there is something else you not want to worry about. And that is baby-sitting. What about club? Do you make decision yet?"

I shifted my position uncomfortably. I was sitting on one kitchen chair with my leg propped up on another.

"No," I replied. "I haven't made a decision."

"You think about it?" Mimi asked me.

"Well, not too much. I've been trying not to."

Mimi nodded. Janine or my parents might have prodded me or scolded me, but Mimi just accepted that I was having some trouble.

I looked at the kitchen clock. Five-fifteen. My friends would be arriving soon, but not soon enough to save me from this discussion. "You know what the problem is?" I said to Mimi. "I don't think I *want* to make a decision. I don't want to baby-sit because I'm afraid to, and I don't want to drop out of the club because I like being part of it. So if I don't make up my mind, I won't have to do either one."

"That is called being in limbo, my Claudia, and you cannot stay there," Mimi informed me gently. She wasn't going to come right out and say it, but she meant that I better make a decision.

"I just can't decide," I told her. "I know I should be able to talk to you or Mom or Dad or Janine — or my friends — but I feel like I can't because there's nothing to say. I don't know how to talk about this anymore. It's not — "

Ring, ring.

"I'll get it," I said. I had chosen my spot in the kitchen carefully. I was close to both the phone and the refrigerator. I could get to either one without moving much. I picked up the receiver. "Hello?"

"Hi!"

"Hi, Stacey! How come you're calling on this line?"

"Because I figured you'd be downstairs. . . . And I was right!"

"Oh. Well, great timing! Everyone's going to be here in a few minutes."

"I know. That's why I called now. I wanted to talk to you, and I figured that by the time we finished, the other girls would have arrived and I could talk to them, too."

"Oh, good. But it'd be easier if I talked to you in my room. So if you don't mind, let me crawl upstairs and I'll call you from my phone. Okay?"

"Okay."

Stacey and I hung up. "Mimi?" I said. "I know I have to make a decision. I know I can't stay in limbo. So I *will* decide. But it might take awhile."

"That is okay, my Claudia. It is okay as long as you are responsible. And making the decision is part of being responsible."

I nodded. Then I got my crutches, hobbled to the stairs, and with Mimi watching anxiously from below, backed awkwardly to the second floor on my bottom, dragging my crutches with me. When I reached my room, I settled on my bed and dialed Stacey.

"Hi," I said. "Okay, I'm in my room now. How are you doing?"

"Fine," Stacey replied. "How are *you?*"

"Bored."

"I bet. Once I missed a whole month of

school. I was so bored my mother said she was going to look for a full-time job. She couldn't take me anymore. Of course, she was kidding. I think."

"Mimi's being really patient," I told Stacey.

"What else *would* Mimi be?" Stacey replied. We laughed.

"Well?" said Stacey.

"Well, what?"

"Well, what are you going to do about the Baby-sitters Club?"

"Oh, my lord. Is that *all* anyone can think of?"

"Excuse me," said Stacey. "It was only a question."

"Sorry. Mimi just asked me about it, too. The answer is, I still don't know."

Stacey and I talked for a few more minutes, and even though that was really great, it made me think how much I miss her. We used to have all the time in the world for talks. Then my friends started to arrive. Dawn and Kristy came first, then Mary Anne, then Mallory, then Jessi. Dawn, Kristy, and Mary Anne each spoke with Stacey.

"I," I said to Jessi and Mallory while the others were crowded around the phone, "will be *so* glad to put on real clothes. You can't imagine. I haven't been dressed in days."

"Do you know what you're going to wear to school on Wednesday?" asked Jessi.

"Not for sure. But it'll have to be a dress. I'm not going to cut slits up the legs of all my pants and jeans, just so I can get them on over my cast. . . . Hey, Mary Anne!" I whispered loudly, tapping her arm. "Get off the phone, okay? This call is costing a fortune."

When Mary Anne had said good-bye, Kristy called the meeting to order. "Our first piece of business," she said, "is that we need an answer, Claud."

"An answer to what?"

"Are you in the club or not?" Kristy asked bluntly.

"What *is* this?" I cried. "Torture Claudia Day? I don't *have* an answer."

"Claud," Dawn said gently, "we don't want you to leave the club. But if you're going to, we need to know."

"Right," agreed Kristy, a little more sympathetically. "I mean, we couldn't keep holding meetings in your room if you weren't a member of the club. So we'd have to find a new meeting place and give our new number to all our clients. We'd have some work to do. That's why we'd kind of like your answer."

I sighed. "I just can't tell you yet. Because I

don't know the answer myself. I'm really sorry. I know it isn't convenient."

"Oh, *Claud*," said Mary Anne, sounding disappointed. "You can't drop out of the club. We've had too much fun. Remember — "

"*This* wasn't fun," I said, pointing to my leg.

"No, of course not. But don't forget about the fun we *have* had. Remember when Lucy Newton was christened?"

"And remember our trip to Disney World?" said Dawn.

"And our trip to New York?" added Kristy.

I glanced at Mal and Jessi, hoping they didn't feel too left out. They hadn't come to New York with us, since they were too young. And they hadn't been part of the club when we went on the other trip.

But they didn't look upset at all, which meant that they probably weren't even thinking about the trips. They just wanted an answer from me, like everyone else did.

"Can I give you my answer in a week?" I asked. "That's all I need. Just one more week."

"Okay," said Kristy. "Sure. Claud, tell us something, though. Do you miss baby-sitting?"

"I miss everything!"

"Honestly. Do you miss it?" she asked seriously.

I paused. "Yes. I do. I'd give anything to see Jamie or Myriah or Gabbie or Karen or one of your sisters or brothers, Mal."

"You're going to stay in the club, I just know you are!" exclaimed Mary Anne.

"I'm really not sure," I said.

We stopped talking then because the phone began ringing. We set up some jobs.

"How's Betsy?" I dared to ask, when we hit a lull.

"The same," replied Mal, sounding irritated. "Joke, joke, joke. We can't beat her. She's unstoppable."

"We're losing the war, aren't we?" I said.

Kristy screwed up her face. "I hate to admit it, but yes. We're losing it."

"That's what I was afraid of," I said thoughtfully. "Mimi is right. We can't control everything in life. And I don't like that."

My friends and I looked at each other. No one said a word. The room was silent.

"Gosh, I'm bored!" I exclaimed. "Anyone have any lint balls? I'll be glad to pick them off your clothes for you."

We all laughed — but I was feeling worried. Now I had only a week to decide if I really wanted to be in the Baby-sitters Club.

CHAPTER 13

Saturday

I did it, I did it, I did it! Just a few
days ago we thought we'd lost the war
against our great practical joker. Today
we won it. Oh, okay, I won't be modest.
I won it. I won the war. I did have a little
help, though. You know how we're always
complaining about Sam because sometimes
he goof-calls us at our meetings? Well,
today my brother and his jokes came through.
Leave it to Sam to be able to out-joke
Betsy Sobak. You want to know how good
he is? This is how good he is. He helped
me out-joke her and he hadn't even been
to the film festival. (He has ordered
from McBuzz's a few times, though.) All
Sam needed to know was that Betsy
and I were going to the movies....

Leave it to *Sam?* No — leave it to Kristy. Kristy and her great ideas. Sam did help her, but Kristy was the one who finally beat Betsy at her own game of jokes. On Saturday, three days after I was allowed to go back to school, Kristy had a special sitting job with Betsy. The movie theater downtown was having a two-week-long run of kids' movies — *Mary Poppins*, *The Parent Trap*, *The Red Balloon*, *The Wizard of Oz*, *Swiss Family Robinson*, all sorts of things. The Saturday afternoon feature was *Chitty Chitty Bang Bang*, and Mrs. Sobak had asked Kristy to take Betsy while she and Mr. Sobak went to another golf tournament. She said she'd buy the tickets and refreshments, then pay Kristy a small fee. (After all, Kristy was getting a free movie out of the deal.)

The movie date was Kristy's first job with Betsy. Kristy saw it as a giant challenge. She wasn't sure she could actually beat Betsy, but she was determined not to lose another battle. As soon as she found out what kind of afternoon had been planned for her and Betsy, she went to her brother Sam. She explained the problem we were having and — bang — just like that, Sam had tons of advice (well, jokes) for Kristy. And they were jokes that would work especially nicely in a movie theater.

*　　*　　*

At twelve o'clock on Saturday afternoon, a car horn honked in front of the Brewer mansion. Kristy ran outside. The Sobaks were waiting in the driveway. She slid into the backseat next to Betsy. Mr. and Mrs. Sobak were in the front.

"Now," said Mrs. Sobak as she drove through Stoneybrook, "the movie starts at twelve-thirty and it's long — almost two and a half hours — so it'll let out just before three. Mr. Sobak and I will be home around five. You two can walk to our house after the movie — it isn't far — and then Kristy, we'll drive you home later. Is that okay?"

"That's fine," replied Kristy, as Betsy sneakily squirted her with her trick fountain pen. Kristy ignored Betsy. She didn't even wipe the water off her face.

The Sobaks let Betsy and Kristy off in front of the movie theater. Mrs. Sobak handed Kristy some money, and then she pulled the car into the stream of traffic on Stoneybrook's main street. "Ta-ta!" she called.

"Okay, Bets," said Kristy. "Get ready for a great movie. And," she went on, "I have something important to tell you. I'd like you to listen carefully."

"Okay," said Betsy curiously, as Kristy pulled

115

her away from the crowd of kids in front of the theater.

"What I want to tell you is . . . no more practical jokes. I won't put up with them," said Kristy firmly. "I don't like them, even if you do. So *no practical jokes*. Got it? Not one more." Kristy had told herself that she would not put her plan into action unless it was really called for. If Betsy was good, then Kristy would not continue the practical-joke war.

"Okay," said Betsy a bit uncertainly.

"I'm not kidding," Kristy told her. "So promise me."

"I promise."

"What do you promise?"

"I promise not to play any more practical jokes," said Betsy obediently.

"All right," Kristy replied.

Betsy flashed Kristy a big smile. "Please can I give the lady the money for our tickets?" Betsy begged. "I just love doing that. I'll say, 'One adult and one child, please.' "

"Sure," said Kristy. "Here you go." She held out some of the money Mrs. Sobak had just given her. Betsy reached for it, and — *BZZZZZZ!*

"Gotcha!" hooted Betsy. "I gotcha with my joy buzzer! Hee-hee-hee!"

I don't believe it! thought Kristy. The kid

played another joke. Right after flat-out promising *not* to. Well, that does it. The plan goes into effect *now*.

Kristy just smiled. Soon she would be the one saying, "Gotcha!"

Betsy and Kristy joined the line of kids waiting to buy tickets. An awful lot of people were standing outside the theater. Kristy looked around, hoping to see someone she knew. But she didn't recognize any faces.

Betsy did, though. "Hey! There are Hilary and Cici!" she whispered to Kristy. "Oh, and Justin and Joey."

"Go say hi," Kristy suggested.

Betsy looked uncomfortable. "Uh, no. That's okay."

"No, really. Go on. I'll save our places in line."

Betsy shook her head. "I don't think they like me."

"Any particular reason?" asked Kristy.

"Maybe because I tied their shoes together during assembly last week. When they stood up, they fell down."

"Well, that'd do it," said Kristy drily.

"And also because I fixed the door to the girls' room so that a baggie full of water fell on Cici when she went inside. . . . Oh, and I put fake ants in Justin's sandwich, and a fake fly in Joey's pudding, and fake barf in Hilary's lunch."

"You put fake *barf* in someone's *lunch?*" exclaimed Kristy. "That's disgusting!"

"I know," said Betsy, who looked both guilty and proud of herself.

"So now those kids don't like you?" asked Kristy.

"I don't think so."

Hmm. Kristy decided to keep her eye on Hilary and Cici and Justin and Joey.

The line was moving fast. Soon Kristy and Betsy and Betsy's classmates had bought their tickets and were entering the theater.

"Can we get popcorn?" asked Betsy.

"Sure," replied Kristy, "but we better find seats first. Come on."

Betsy chose seats in almost the exact center of the theater. Her classmates sat on the other side of the aisle, several rows behind. As soon as Betsy and Kristy had taken off their jackets and settled down, Betsy said, "*Now* can I get popcorn? And can I go by myself, please? I know just where to go. I promise I'll go straight to the refreshment stand and come straight back."

"Okay, if you *promise,*" said Kristy, who was thinking, This is great! This is perfect! This is better than perfect, joke-wise. But all she said was, "Here's some more money. Why don't you get a large box of popcorn?"

"Okay!" cried Betsy. "Goody."

"Now, hurry," Kristy added as Betsy edged down the row. "The movie is going to start in about five minutes."

Betsy rushed away. Kristy watched her. As soon as Betsy was out of sight, Kristy stood up, grabbed the jackets, hurried to the aisle, and moved six rows back. The theater was filling up fast, but she found two empty seats on the aisle. Then she leaned back and tried to look nonchalant.

Right across the aisle were Hilary, Cici, Justin, and Joey. They were giggling and fooling around. The boys were tossing popcorn in the air and catching it in their mouths.

Smirking to herself, Kristy watched the aisle for Betsy. When the lights began to dim and there was no sign of Betsy, she felt slightly nervous. She remembered how Betsy had hidden from Mallory.

And then, suddenly, there was Betsy. The theater was almost dark and the curtain was rising in front of the movie screen. But the aisle was lit with tiny lights, so Kristy was able to watch Betsy as she marched past her, clutching the popcorn. Betsy slowed down as she approached the middle of the theater. Kristy

119

knew she was searching for her own empty seat. But there were no empty seats now — except for the one next to Kristy. The theater was full.

Betsy paused. She looked around. She walked to the front of the theater. She walked back. "Kristy?" she whispered loudly.

Across the aisle from Kristy, Justin nudged Joey and pointed at Betsy. "Look!" he said. "It's Betsy the brat!"

Joey snorted rudely.

"Kristy!" Betsy whispered again. "Kristy, where are you?"

Kristy kept her mouth shut. She knew Betsy was safe as long as she was within her view.

"KRISTY?"

"SHHH!" said several people.

Hilary and Cici giggled.

"SHHH!" said someone else.

"KRISTY?"

Okay. Enough was enough. "Over here, Bets," Kristy whispered loudly. She waved to Betsy.

Betsy finally saw Kristy. She marched over to her and plopped down in the empty seat. Her classmates were hooting and giggling. "Kristy, Kristy, help me!" Justin was saying in a high voice.

"You switched seats!" Betsy said accusingly to Kristy.

"Gotcha!" Kristy replied.

Betsy sulked. But not for long. The movie had started and the popcorn was good. It's difficult to stay mad under those conditions.

Kristy decided to put the next part of her plan into action. She wasn't going to let up on Betsy. Not while things were going so well. And not after all the jokes Betsy had played on the members of the Baby-sitters Club. And *especially* not after promising Kristy she wouldn't play any more jokes.

"Why don't you let me hold the popcorn for awhile?" Kristy asked Betsy. "I'll keep it right here between us. Your hand must be getting tired."

"Yeah. Thanks," said Betsy gratefully.

Kristy held the box with her left hand. Her right hand was busily working its way into her pocket. It closed over something that Sam had lent her. Kristy pulled it out and slipped it onto her left thumb. Then carefully, quietly, she worked her thumb through the flap on the bottom of the popcorn box.

Betsy never noticed a thing.

The movie continued. The popcorn was disappearing fast, although Kristy had stopped eating it. Betsy was the only one whose hand was going back and forth from her mouth to the box.

On the screen, Chitty Chitty Bang Bang, the wonderful car, took to the air for the first time. As it flew, the kids in the theater cheered.

Betsy reached into the popcorn box again. This time, Kristy felt Betsy's fingers brush her thumb. Betsy paused in her eating. She rustled her hand around in the box. Her hand closed over Kristy's thumb. Betsy drew in her breath sharply. Then she leaned over and peered inside the box.

There was just enough light for her to see what appeared to be mixed in with the popcorn she'd been eating — a large, bruised, bloody thumb. Considering that the fake thumb had come from McBuzz's, so Betsy had probably seen it a hundred times in the catalogue — and maybe even owned one — Kristy was surprised that Betsy screamed as loudly as she did. It must have been, Kristy told me later, the element of surprise.

"AUGHHH!" shrieked Betsy. "AUGHHH!"

"SHHH!" said about thirty-five people around Kristy and Betsy.

Kristy didn't let the gag go on for too long. She pulled her thumb out of the box and took off the fake one. Then she held it up for Betsy to see.

"Gotcha again," she said.

From across the aisle came giggles and snickers. Cici, Hilary, Justin, and Joey took great pleasure in seeing the practical-joke queen outjoked.

"Why'd you do that?" Betsy whispered angrily to Kristy. "I am *so* embarrassed."

"Well, remember that the next time you think about playing a joke on someone else. And why did I do it? I did it because you gave Claudia pepper gum, you hid from Mallory, you made Dawn eat shaving cream, and you squirted me with your pen."

"And you put barf in my lunch," said a voice from across the aisle.

An usher appeared next to Betsy. "If you kids can't keep quiet," she said, "I'll have to ask you to leave. People are complaining. Settle down, please."

When the usher was gone, Kristy whispered as softly as possible, "Do you want to stay for the rest of the movie, Betsy?"

"Yes," she replied.

"SHHH!"

So they stayed. Betsy barely moved a muscle until the movie was over and the lights came on again.

CHAPTER 14

When her eyes had adjusted to the light, Kristy looked over at Betsy. Betsy was staring straight ahead. She was studiously ignoring her classmates who, as they put on their jackets, kept saying things, like, "Oh! Oh, save me!" and "Eek! There's a bloody thumb in my popcorn!"

When they had left, Kristy said gently, "Come on, Betsy. We have to go now. Put your jacket on."

Betsy was obedient. She put her jacket on silently as people pushed along next to her, jamming the aisle.

After a few moments, Betsy looked over at Kristy and said, "I know the real reason you tricked me. It was because of Claudia's leg, right?"

"Well, Claudia was certainly the only one who really got hurt from one of your jokes — "

124

"But I — " Betsy interrupted.

"I know. I know you didn't mean for her to get hurt, but she did anyway. And other people could have gotten hurt from your jokes. What if the shaving cream had made Dawn sick? What if one of your rubber toys had frightened someone so much that she fainted? Or fell? When you set people up, Betsy, you don't know what might happen. Furthermore," (the theater was emptying, and Kristy and Betsy edged into the aisle), "furthermore," Kristy said again, "sometimes your jokes are funny, but most of the time they embarrass people. The jokes make them feel the way you felt today when I tricked you."

Betsy nodded. She didn't seem quite so mad anymore. But she was awfully subdued. As they left the theater and walked into the sunlight, she said worriedly, "How *is* Claudia?"

"She's doing pretty well. She was finally allowed to go back to school last Wednesday."

"Just last Wednesday?" Betsy sounded shocked. "But she broke her leg months ago!"

Kristy laughed. "No, just three and a half weeks — well, almost one month ago." She paused. "That's hard to believe."

"Is she going to be all right?" asked Betsy in a small voice.

Kristy suddenly realized that Betsy had probably been feeling awfully guilty about me. Maybe . . . maybe that was why Betsy had continued to play jokes after the accident — to prove to herself that her tricks couldn't *really* hurt anyone, that my accident had been, well, just an accident.

"Betsy," said Kristy, coming to a stop, "would you like to see Claudia? We could go over to her house right now, if we turn around and head in the other direction. It's not too far away. Then we can walk to your house after we visit her. Maybe you'd, um, like to talk to Claudia and tell her you're sorry."

"Okay," said Betsy in a *very* small voice.

When our doorbell rang, I was in the living room with my dad and Janine. They were trying to help me study for a math test that was coming up on Monday. But I wasn't being very cooperative. I just kept putting my head in my hands and moaning, "I can't learn this! I've missed too much school."

Ding-dong.

I actually cried, "Oh, goody! The doorbell."

Dad and my sister shook their heads.

"I'll get it," I added as I grabbed my crutches and hobbled to the front door.

Believe me, Kristy and Betsy were the last two people I expected to find standing on our stoop. I'd been hoping for a visit from Mary Anne and Tigger, or the Perkins girls, or maybe a cute boy who was concerned about my recovery. (I wasn't picky. Any cute boy would do.)

"Hi," said Betsy sheepishly.

"Hi," I replied. "I got your note." Betsy had written me a note of apology while I was in the hospital.

Betsy nodded. "My daddy fixed the swing," she told me.

Kristy cleared her throat. "Could we come in?" she asked.

"Oh. Oh, sure. Sorry about that." I moved aside and let Kristy and Betsy in.

"I think Betsy wants to talk to you in private," Kristy whispered to me as she went by, and saw Dad and Janine in the living room.

"Okay." I tried to think where we could go. It was such a production getting to my bedroom, but in the end, that's where we went. At least, with Dad and Janine and Kristy around I was allowed to hop up the stairs with my crutches instead of backing up on my bottom.

I settled myself on my bed, Betsy sat cautiously next to me, and Kristy took her usual place in my director's chair.

"I want to tell you something," Betsy said.

"I want to say that I'm sorry. I mean, I know I wrote that in the note, but I want to say it, too. Because I really mean it. Kristy said you're going to be okay. You are, aren't you?"

"Yes. But not for awhile. I'm not done wearing the cast, and even after it's off I'll have to have physical therapy. You know, exercise and stuff." Betsy was looking pretty worried, so I added, "But, hey! The hospital was kind of fun. I got tons of attention — flowers, cards, visitors."

Betsy gave me a tiny smile.

"Tell Claudia what happened in the theater today," Kristy spoke up.

"Kristy tricked me," said Betsy. She looked down at my bedspread, tracing the pattern of the fabric with her finger.

"And?" Kristy prompted her.

"And it was really awful. I was so embarrassed. . . . Did I embarrass you, Claudia?" she asked.

Betsy's question took me by surprise. I hadn't really thought about it. "Well, yes," I told her. "I guess you did."

"I'm sorry about that, too, then," said Betsy.

"Hey, don't feel so bad," I said. I reached behind my pillow and pulled out a bag of Tootsie Rolls. "Here, have one." I handed a Tootsie Roll to Betsy.

She looked at it warily.

"It isn't a trick!" I said, exasperated. "You know, if *you* didn't play so many tricks, you wouldn't have to worry about *other* people wanting to trick you back. Wouldn't that be nice?"

Betsy nodded. Then she unwrapped the candy and ate it. When she had finished, she smiled. "Thanks, Claudia."

"Thank *you*. I'm glad you came over."

"We better get going," said Kristy. "Claud, I'll be back after the Sobaks come home. I want to talk to you. When I get here, I'll call Charlie and ask him to come pick me up. Is that okay?"

"Sure," I replied.

Kristy and Betsy left. An hour and a half later, Kristy returned. Instead of heading for the director's chair, she sat with me on my bed. She picked up a Magic Marker and doodled on my cast.

"Your week is almost up," she informed me. "On Monday you have to give us your decision about staying in the club. Do you know what you're going to say? I don't mean to be pushy," Kristy rushed on, "but I *am* the club president, so I feel it's my duty to talk to you about this."

"That's okay," I told her. "The funny thing is, up until Betsy came over, I did think I knew what I was going to say. I was going to tell you that sitting is too risky and I was dropping out."

"*Really?*" Kristy was wide-eyed.

I nodded. "But something Betsy said this afternoon — "

"About her trick embarrassing you?"

"Yeah. How did you know?"

Kristy shrugged.

"Well, I started thinking," I continued. "I *was* embarrassed. Humiliated, too, I guess. But I didn't want to admit it, so I started, what's the word? Oh, yeah. I started focusing on all the other stuff. But the plain truth is — I was embarrassed. And that's no reason to quit the club."

"Wasn't there something else, too?" asked Kristy. "Something Mimi said?"

"Oh, yeah. About control. She said we can't control everything in our lives. I think she means that I could, like, stop baby-sitting, but that wouldn't keep me from having an accident on my bike or in gym class, or from falling down the stairs, you know? Plus, when I was thinking about things this afternoon, I realized something else. We've baby-sat for a *lot* of kids since the club started and nothing like this has ever happened. We haven't run into any other kids like Betsy. She's the only one. Also, one time Ashley pointed out how many extra art classes I could take if I weren't sitting, but I didn't feel cheered up and I think now I know why. If I weren't sitting, I'd just plain miss the kids — a lot."

"So?" said Kristy, smiling. "Are you saying you're in the club?"

"Yup — as long as I don't have to sit for Betsy again. I just don't think I could do it. Is that okay?"

"It's fine! It's great!" Kristy cried. "Let's call everyone else and tell them. I can't wait until Monday."

So we started making phone calls.

First we called Mary Anne. "I knew it!" she cried. "Oh, I'm so happy, Claud!"

Then we called Dawn. "Good going! All right!" she exclaimed.

Then we called Mallory. Claire answered the phone and shouted, "It's for you, Mallory-silly-billy-goo-goo!" (Claire must have been in one of her silly moods.) Mallory got on and said, "Fantastic!"

Then we called Jessi. "Hey, terrific!" she cried.

Last (but certainly not least), we called Stacey.

"Hello," I said. "Is this the New York branch of the Baby-sitters Club?"

Stacey giggled. "Hi, Claud."

"Hi. Guess what. I have news."

"Good or bad?"

"Good."

"Oh, then I know what it is. You're staying in the club, right?"

"Right."

"Congratulations, vice-president! You'd be hard to replace."

"Thanks, Stace."

We talked for a little bit and then I hung up the phone. "Oops," I said to Kristy. "I've got just one more call to make."

The call was to Ashley. I gave her the news.

"You're crazy," she said. But she didn't sound mad.

"I better go," Kristy said to me a few minutes later.

"Okay," I replied. "Help me down the stairs, will you? I want to tell the news to one last person."

"Mimi?" guessed Kristy.

"You got it!"

I was a true club member again. Boy, did it feel great!

CHAPTER 15

Bzzzz. BZZZZ.

"Oh! Oh, that looks awful," I said to my mother. It was two months later and I was back at the hospital. "I can't go through with it. I just can't. I've decided I'll live with my cast. I'll get used to it."

My mother laughed gently. "Relax, Claudia," she told me. "The doctors know what they're doing. They take casts off every day. I bet they haven't lost a limb yet."

"That's comforting, Mom."

A nurse walked by us. "Excuse me," I said. He paused. "Yes?"

"How safe are those gigantic buzz saws? The ones that look like they could slice through a redwood tree without any trouble?" I asked.

The man laughed. "Safe as anything. We haven't lost a limb yet."

As the nurse walked away, my mother turned

to me with raised eyebrows. "What did I tell you?" she said.

"You told me a grown-up thing," I replied. "It's like adults have a stock of jokes and sayings, and they pull one of them out whenever they're trying to cover up for something. They all know which ones to say when. It must be something you learn when you're about twenty-one."

My mother and I were sitting in the fracture clinic in the hospital. It was a place I had come to know very well. After I left the hospital, I had to go to the clinic once every week or two to have my leg X-rayed and my cast checked. I never did get a walking cast, but now my big, nonwalking cast was about to come off for good. It seemed as if it had been part of my body (a very heavy part) forever. It was fully decorated — there wasn't a white patch on it — but I wouldn't miss it a bit. If I could live through having it removed.

I was watching two other people have their casts taken off. One was an old woman (she looked older than Mimi) who'd broken her ankle. The other was a guy about Charlie Thomas' age with a broken arm. A doctor was standing over each of them with a buzz saw. No kidding, the buzz saws had whirling metal disks, which made a tremendous noise, and the disks were slicing through each cast like a pizza cutter slicing through a pie with everything on it. Now, as far as I know, there is nothing between the cast and your bare skin. How do those buzz saws know when to stop?

I watched both procedures. I felt more and more nervous. Nobody shed any blood, though. Still, when the nurse called my name, I said, "That's okay. I've changed my mind. I'm going to keep the cast. I don't want it, but I'll keep it."

"*Claudia,*" said my mother.

The nurse chuckled. "On the table," he commanded.

I got to my feet (well, my foot) slowly.

"Go *on,*" said Mom.

I hobbled over to the table and the nurse helped me lie down on it. Soon a doctor approached me. "Hi, there," he said. "Claudia, right?"

"Right."

There are about six doctors in the fracture clinic, and you never know which one will be treating you. This one was Dr. Rivera.

"Ready for the torture chamber?" he teased me.

I groaned. A comedian. "Oh, lord," I said under my breath.

"If you prop yourself up on your elbows," he said, "you can watch."

Watch? Was he crazy? It would be like watching the dentist pull your tooth out. "No, thanks," I said.

"You're sure?"

"Very, very positive." Now that I was lying there, waiting, I just wanted Dr. Rivera to get on with things. "Mom?" I called. My mother stepped over to me. She took my hand. I hadn't asked her to, but that was just what I needed and she knew it.

"Okay, now," said Dr. Rivera, "you're going to hear a loud noise," (duh) "and feel some vibration and some pressure, but that's all. I promise this won't hurt a bit."

Yeah, right. Having my leg cut off was going to be a picnic.

I closed my eyes.

BZZZ. Dr. Rivera had turned on the buzz saw. All I could picture was a scene from this really old movie. A pretty young woman was tied to a moving belt in a factory where a huge saw cut trees into logs. The belt was inching closer to the saw. . . . The lady was going to be sliced right in half! But of course the hero came along just in time, stopped the machinery, and saved the woman whom he would probably marry some — "AUGHHH!" I shouted.

"Claudia!" cried my mother, just as the doctor said firmly, "Hold still!"

"But I can feel it!" I cried. "It's right next to my skin! The blade is hot. Another eighth of an inch and it'll be too late!"

"The blade is just warm from friction," Dr. Rivera assured me. "Don't worry about it. Claudia, I've taken off hundreds of casts. I know exactly how deep to cut. But if you move, I might slip."

Oh, thank you. Thank you so much for saying that, I thought.

BZZZZ. BZZZZ. The saw was moving along my leg. It was —

"All done!" announced Dr. Rivera. And then I did prop myself up, just in time to see him crack my cast open as if it were a lobster claw. The doctor hadn't cut me. He really did know what he was doing.

"Now don't move your leg at all, Claudia," he said. He pulled the two halves of the cast away. "Want these for souvenirs?" he asked.

"Uh, no, that's okay," I replied. The doctor tossed them into a bin full of other sliced-off casts. "Well, can I go now?" I asked hopefully.

"Sorry, Claudia. I'm afraid you can't just

hop off the table and walk out of the hospital. Your leg would never support you. We've still got a little work to do." I took a close look at my leg and gasped. "What happened?" I cried. My leg looked as thin as a stick — and as limp as a dishrag.

"You haven't used the muscles of this leg in a long time," the doctor explained. "But you'll be surprised at how fast it will look normal again."

"How am I supposed to walk on it?" I exclaimed.

"Oh, you're not. Not for awhile."

Boy, what an ordeal this was. Dr. Rivera splinted my leg. He wrapped an ace bandage around it. Then he handed my crutches to me. "Come back in two days to see the physical therapist," he told me. "And don't walk on that leg before then, understand?"

I did, but I was disappointed. I'd thought the cast would come off and I'd be as good as new. However, I felt a lot better just a little while later. That was because I got home just in time for a meeting of the Baby-sitters Club.

My friends were in rare form.

Dawn had discovered junk jewelry (*real* junk) and was busy making a necklace for herself out of paper clips and colored rubber bands. While she worked on it, Mary Anne sat behind her (they were on the floor) and played with her hair.

"Your hair is longer than Claudia's, you know," she told her. "You should braid it or something."

Jessi and Mallory were making origami swans out of notebook paper.

I just sat and watched. Mostly, I watched Kristy, who was watching everyone else. "Would you guys please come to order?" she finally cried.

"But Kristy," said Mary Anne, not taking her eyes off Dawn's hair, "we've taken care of business and no calls are coming in."

Ring, ring.

"Oh, yeah?" said Kristy. She reached for the phone. "Hello, Baby-sitters Club. No, this isn't Angelo's House of Pizza. I just said it was the Baby — Sam, is that you? . . . It *is!* I am now going to hang up on you," she announced. "You're tying up our line." *Clunk.*

I tried not to laugh.

"Don't we have *any* business?" asked Kristy.

"I have some information," Jessi spoke up. "When I sat for Betsy Sobak last Saturday, guess what I found in her room."

"McBuzz's?" I asked.

Jessi shook her head. "Nope. Something called Squirmy's House of Tricks 'n' Jokes."

"Another catalogue!" I exclaimed, dismayed. "Didn't she learn *any*thing?"

"Well, she might have," said Jessi. "She didn't play a single joke on me."

The phone rang again. This time I answered it. "Hi, Mrs. Barrett," I said. "You need a sitter when?" I began to feel excited. "Okay, I'll get right back to you." I hung up. Then, "Guess what!" I screeched.

I sounded so excited that Jessi and Mallory dropped their swans, Dawn dropped her paper clips, and Mary Anne dropped Dawn's hair.

"What?" they all said.

"Mrs. Barrett needs a sitter, but not until three weeks from Saturday. I'll be able to sit then. I'm sure of it. Please, can I have the job? I know we're not supposed to take a job just because we've answered the phone, but I haven't baby-sat for so long, and I really miss kids."

My friends grinned. And Kristy said, "The job is yours. Go ahead."

I called Mrs. Barrett back while Mary Anne noted the job in our appointment book.

"Boy," I said after I'd hung up, "does this ever feel great. I am so glad I'm still in the club!"

Ring, ring. Since I was so excited, I answered the phone again. "No, this is NOT the Puppy

Parlor. And I do NOT need my poodle clipped!"
I said. Then I added, "Good-bye, Sam," and
hung up.

Kristy looked thoughtful. "You know," she
said, "we have had a *major* problem with
practical jokes lately. And Sam won't quit goof-
calling us, but . . ."

"Yeah?" I prompted her.

"I *still* wouldn't mind getting hit in the face
with a pie!"

I sighed happily. Everything was back to
normal.

Dear Reader:

In *Claudia and the Bad Joke*, trouble starts when Betsy Sobak is carried away by the practical jokes she receives from McBuzz's Mail Order. When I was young, I loved to order things through the mail — from the backs of cereal boxes, from comic books, and, best of all, from bubblegum wrappers. My prize possession was a piece of fool's gold, which came in a little gray flannel sack. It cost twenty-five cents, but I thought it was very valuable.

Back then, hardly any catalogues came in the mail. But every fall, Sears Roebuck sent out its Christmas catalogue, *The Wish Book*. I pored through it, turning down the corners of pages on which I saw toys I wanted. Today, I still do most of my shopping through catalogues. I just love getting things in the mail, although it's been a long time since I ordered a practical joke.

Happy reading,

Ann M. Martin

Ann M. Martin

About the Author

ANN MATTHEWS MARTIN was born on August 12, 1955. She grew up in Princeton, NJ, with her parents and her younger sister, Jane.

Although Ann used to be a teacher and then an editor of children's books, she's now a full-time writer. She gets the ideas for her books from many different places. Some are based on personal experiences. Others are based on childhood memories and feelings. Many are written about contemporary problems or events.

All of Ann's characters, even the members of the Baby-sitters Club, are made up. (So is Stoneybrook.) But many of her characters are based on real people. Sometimes Ann names her characters after people she knows, other times she chooses names she likes.

In addition to the Baby-sitters Club books, Ann Martin has written many other books for children. Her favorite is *Ten Kids, No Pets* because she loves big families and she loves animals. Her favorite Baby-sitters Club book is *Kristy's Big Day*. (By the way, Kristy is her favorite baby-sitter!)

Ann M. Martin now lives in New York with her cats, Gussie and Woody. Her hobbies are reading, sewing, and needlework — especially making clothes for children.

Notebook Pages

This Baby-sitters Club book belongs to _____ .

I am _____ years old and in the _____

grade.

The name of my school is _____ .

I got this BSC book from _____ .

I started reading it on _____ and

finished reading it on _____ .

The place where I read most of this book is _____ .

My favorite part was when _____ .

If I could change anything in the story, it might be the part when

_____ .

My favorite character in the Baby-sitters Club is _____ .

The BSC member I am most like is _____

because _____ .

If I could write a Baby-sitters Club book it would be about ____

_____ .

#19 Claudia and the Bad Joke

Betsy Sobak playes a bad joke on Claudia, which causes Claudia to break her leg. The worst joke someone ever played on me was when _____

_____. The worst joke that I ever played on someone was when _____

_____. The best joke I ever played was when _____

_____. The person I know who plays the best jokes is _____. If I could play a joke on someone right now, it would be _____ because _____

_____

_____. The best joke I know, but have never tried, is

_____. After Claudia is hurt by Betsy's bad joke, she has to go to the hospital. The worst accident I've ever had was when _____

_____. After I had this accident, I had to

_____

_____.

CLAUDIA'S

Finger painting at 3...

A spooky sitting advent

Sitting for two of my favorite charges --
Jamie and Lucy Newton.

SCRAPBOOK

...oil painting
at 13!

my family. Mom and Dad, me and
Janine... and we'll never forget Mimi.

Read all the books
about **Claudia**
in the Baby-sitters Club series
by Ann M. Martin

2 *Claudia and the Phantom Phone Calls*
Someone mysterious is calling Claudia!

7 *Claudia and Mean Janine*
Claudia's big sister is super smart . . . and super
mean.

#12 *Claudia and the New Girl*
Claudia might give up the club — and it's all Ashley's fault.

#19 *Claudia and the Bad Joke*
When Claudia baby-sits for a practical joker, she's
headed for big trouble.

#26 *Claudia and the Sad Good-bye*
Claudia never thought anything bad would happen to her grandmother, Mimi.

#33 *Claudia and the Great Search*
Claudia thinks she was adopted — and no one
told her about it.

#40 *Claudia and the Middle School Mystery*
How could anyone accuse *Claudia* of cheating?

#49 *Claudia and the Genius of Elm Street*
Baby-sitting for a seven-year-old genius makes
Claudia feel like a world-class dunce.

#56 *Keep Out, Claudia!*
Who wouldn't want Claudia for a baby-sitter?

#63 *Claudia's Fr~~ien~~d Friend*
Claudia and Shea can't spell — but they can be friends!

#78 *Claudia and Crazy Peaches*
Claudia's Crazy Aunt Peaches is back in town. Let the games begin!

#85 *Claudia Kishi, Live From WSTO!*
Claudia wins a contest to have her own radio show.

#91 *Claudia and the First Thanksgiving*
Claudia's in the middle of a big Thanksgiving controversy!

Mysteries:

6 *The Mystery at Claudia's House*
Claudia's room has been ransacked! Can the Baby-sitters track down whodunnit?

#11 *Claudia and the Mystery at the Museum*
Burglaries, forgeries . . . something crooked is going on at the new museum in Stoneybrook!

#16 *Claudia and the Clue in the Photograph*
Has Claudia caught a thief — on film?

#21 *Claudia and the Recipe for Danger*
There's nothing half-baked about the attempts to sabotage a big cooking contest!

Portrait Collection:

Claudia's Book
Claudia's design for living.

THE BABY-SITTERS CLUB®

by Ann M. Martin

❏ MG43388-1	#1	Kristy's Great Idea	$3.50
❏ MG43387-3	#10	Logan Likes Mary Anne!	$3.50
❏ MG43717-8	#15	Little Miss Stoneybrook and Dawn	$3.50
❏ MG43722-4	#20	Kristy and the Walking Disaster	$3.50
❏ MG43347-4	#25	Mary Anne and the Search for Tigger	$3.50
❏ MG42498-X	#30	Mary Anne and the Great Romance	$3.50
❏ MG42508-0	#35	Stacey and the Mystery of Stoneybrook	$3.50
❏ MG44082-9	#40	Claudia and the Middle School Mystery	$3.25
❏ MG43574-4	#45	Kristy and the Baby Parade	$3.50
❏ MG44969-9	#50	Dawn's Big Date	$3.50
❏ MG44968-0	#51	Stacey's Ex-Best Friend	$3.50
❏ MG44966-4	#52	Mary Anne + 2 Many Babies	$3.50
❏ MG44967-2	#53	Kristy for President	$3.25
❏ MG44965-6	#54	Mallory and the Dream Horse	$3.25
❏ MG44964-8	#55	Jessi's Gold Medal	$3.25
❏ MG45657-1	#56	Keep Out, Claudia!	$3.50
❏ MG45658-X	#57	Dawn Saves the Planet	$3.50
❏ MG45659-8	#58	Stacey's Choice	$3.50
❏ MG45660-1	#59	Mallory Hates Boys (and Gym)	$3.50
❏ MG45662-8	#60	Mary Anne's Makeover	$3.50
❏ MG45663-6	#61	Jessi's and the Awful Secret	$3.50
❏ MG45664-4	#62	Kristy and the Worst Kid Ever	$3.50
❏ MG45665-2	#63	Claudia's Friend	$3.50
❏ MG45666-0	#64	Dawn's Family Feud	$3.50
❏ MG45667-9	#65	Stacey's Big Crush	$3.50
❏ MG47004-3	#66	Maid Mary Anne	$3.50
❏ MG47005-1	#67	Dawn's Big Move	$3.50
❏ MG47006-X	#68	Jessi and the Bad Baby-Sitter	$3.50
❏ MG47007-8	#69	Get Well Soon, Mallory!	$3.50
❏ MG47008-6	#70	Stacey and the Cheerleaders	$3.50
❏ MG47009-4	#71	Claudia and the Perfect Boy	$3.50
❏ MG47010-8	#72	Dawn and the We Love Kids Club	$3.50

More titles... ▶

❑ MG47011-6	#73 Mary Anne and Miss Priss	$3.50
❑ MG47012-4	#74 Kristy and the Copycat	$3.50
❑ MG47013-2	#75 Jessi's Horrible Prank	$3.50
❑ MG47014-0	#76 Stacey's Lie	$3.50
❑ MG48221-1	#77 Dawn and Whitney, Friends Forever	$3.50
❑ MG48222-X	#78 Claudia and Crazy Peaches	$3.50
❑ MG48223-8	#79 Mary Anne Breaks the Rules	$3.50
❑ MG48224-6	#80 Mallory Pike, #1 Fan	$3.50
❑ MG48225-4	#81 Kristy and Mr. Mom	$3.50
❑ MG48226-2	#82 Jessi and the Troublemaker	$3.50
❑ MG48235-1	#83 Stacey vs. the BSC	$3.50
❑ MG48228-9	#84 Dawn and the School Spirit War	$3.50
❑ MG48236-X	#85 Claudi Kishi, Live from WSTO	$3.50
❑ MG48227-0	#86 Mary Anne and Camp BSC	$3.50
❑ MG48237-8	#87 Stacey and the Bad Girls	$3.50
❑ MG22872-2	#88 Farewell, Dawn	$3.50
❑ MG22873-0	#89 Kristy and the Dirty Diapers	$3.50
❑ MG45575-3	Logan's Story Special Edition Readers' Request	$3.25
❑ MG47118-X	Logan Bruno, Boy Baby-sitter Special Edition Readers' Request	$3.50
❑ MG47756-0	Shannon's Story Special Edition	$3.50
❑ MG44240-6	Baby-sitters on Board! Super Special #1	$3.95
❑ MG44239-2	Baby-sitters' Summer Vacation Super Special #2	$3.95
❑ MG43973-1	Baby-sitters' Winter Vacation Super Special #3	$3.95
❑ MG42493-9	Baby-sitters' Island Adventure Super Special #4	$3.95
❑ MG43575-2	California Girls! Super Special #5	$3.95
❑ MG43576-0	New York, New York! Super Special #6	$3.95
❑ MG44963-X	Snowbound Super Special #7	$3.95
❑ MG44962-X	Baby-sitters at Shadow Lake Super Special #8	$3.95
❑ MG45661-X	Starring the Baby-sitters Club Super Special #9	$3.95
❑ MG45674-1	Sea City, Here We Come! Super Special #10	$3.95
❑ MG47015-9	The Baby-sitter's Remember Super Special #11	$3.95
❑ MG48308-0	Here Come the Bridesmaids Super Special #12	$3.95

Available wherever you buy books...or use this order form.

Scholastic Inc., P.O. Box 7502, 2931 E. McCarty Street, Jefferson City, MO 65102

Please send me the books I have checked above. I am enclosing $ _____
(please add $2.00 to cover shipping and handling). Send check or money order—no
cash or C.O.D.s please.

Name _____ Birthdate _____

Address _____

City _____ State/Zip _____

Please allow four to six weeks for delivery. Offer good in the U.S. only. Sorry, mail orders are not
available to residents of Canada. Prices subject to change.